Andria Reingold-McLaughlin is an artist, educator, and writer who resides on Long Island. Since receiving her M.A. in communication arts and an M.S. in school counseling, she has worked in a public school, teaching art to students from kindergarten through twelfth grade. She has two boys, Tyler and Aaron, who continue to inspire her to write stories about children with a voice, strength, and intelligence.

To my children who will always be my inspiration and will continue to keep me on my toes.
I love you!

Andria Reingold-McLaughlin

CHILDREN OF THE AMAZON

AUSTIN MACAULEY PUBLISHERS™

LONDON · CAMBRIDGE · NEW YORK · SHARJAH

Ordering Information:
Quantity sales: special discounts are available on quantity purchases by corporations, associations, and others. For details, contact the publisher at the address below.

Publisher's Cataloging-in-Publication data
Reingold-McLaughlin, Andria
Children of the Amazon

ISBN 9781643784496 (Paperback)
ISBN 9781643784502 (Hardback)
ISBN 9781645367840 (ePub e-book)

Library of Congress Control Number: 2019917074

www.austinmacauley.com/us

First Published (2020)
Austin Macauley Publishers LLC
40 Wall Street, 28th Floor
New York, NY 10005
USA

mail-usa@austinmacauley.com
+1 (646) 5125767

Jeanne Agnello: thank you for your time, your patience, and your encouragement.
Julieta McLaughlin: thank you for sharing your beautiful stories and your Brazilian culture with our family.

Chapter 1

Dreams

The waterfall danced on the rocks and poured into a pond that rippled under my fingertips. I cleaned my hands and washed the grit from under my nails. Sweat rolled down the side of my cheek, so I splashed my face with the water again and again until I felt cool. I was tired and my body ached. When the water cleared, I leaned over to peer into the pool and caught a glimpse of a woman looking back at me. It was then I realized how beautiful my mother was. I woke up, gasping for air.

My hands trembled. I reached for the lamp, missed the cord, and nearly fell out of bed. I realized that it had been a dream, but it all felt so real! My room was dark and I was still disoriented. The glow of light seeped in from under the door and I was comforted. My father managed to push his way through the doorway in spite of the clothes that had been strewn about.

"Everything okay, honey?"

"Yes." I lay back on my pillow and closed my eyes.

"Are you sure? I heard you cry," he said.

"I… I saw Mom. I think she's in trouble."

He looked around at the mess in my room and wrinkled his nose in disgust. "It was just a dream, Larissa. Go back to sleep," he said. My father's response was exactly what I had expected: distant, disbelieving.

"No Dad, it wasn't just a dream. Call Mom. See if she's alright." My voice grew louder.

"Shhh." He put his finger to his lips. "You'll wake your brother," he whispered. "I spoke to Mom a few hours ago. She's fine. Now get some sleep."

My father pulled down my red window shade, sighed, and glanced around my bedroom again. I waited for his usual comments about the mess, but he left my room without a word. His footsteps echoed through the hall and grew quieter as he slipped into his bedroom. I shut my eyes tight and found that I had twirled my hair into a knot, something I did when I was nervous. He didn't believe me again!

The problem with being a teenager is that adults never listen. They always *say* they are listening, but they really aren't. I knew that something was wrong with my mother. I felt it. She was in some kind of trouble and I was the only one who could see her through my dream.

My mother was the only exception. She believed me when I told her that some of the dreams I'd had were real premonitions of the future. She stopped whatever she was doing. She could be in the middle of washing the dishes or reading the mail. She had once logged off the computer while she was working, just to hear about my dreams. They had begun about a year or so before, and I noticed that an event would take place one day after I dreamed about it. I didn't believe it myself at first until I dreamed about a pipe that burst in the bathroom. The next day, our bathroom was flooded. I wasn't totally convinced, so I began to write details of my dreams in a journal, something my mother had suggested. She was intrigued by my entries. She called it *"poderes,"* which meant "powers" in Portuguese. My father remained skeptical. It was his nature to be that way. I knew he was still curious though, as he read each journal entry and waited to see if my next prediction of a future event would occur. The dreams stopped for a while until this one dream. This felt real.

By morning, I hadn't remembered much until the phone rang. The imagery flooded back as soon as I heard my father say *"oi,"* which meant "hello" in Portuguese. I tried to listen to the voice on the other end of the receiver. I was always able to hear better than most people, picking up on faint whispers and distant noises. Mom warned me that these abilities require a significant amount of respect for others' privacy. I guessed she was worried that I would listen in on another person's conversation, a task that was often difficult to avoid. No matter what, I couldn't understand more than a word or two of Portuguese, so I stopped eavesdropping.

My father listened for quite a while before he spoke. His face was very serious and he nodded occasionally. He asked dozens of questions in English about my mother and her work, the last person she had spoken to, and her most recent journal entries. I was watching his expressions to get some idea of what was happening but he just nodded and muttered *"obrigado,"* which meant "thank you," and hung up the phone. He called my little brother Sergio to the table.

"That was the Brazilian police. There was an accident." He swallowed, looking down at his hands, which were trembling now. "They suspect that Mom's prop plane went down somewhere in the Amazon. The police sent out a search party. They said they'd inform us every few hours if they should find anything." There was a long pause. We waited for something more but the air was thick with silence.

"How do they know the plane went down?" Sergio asked. "She could have landed safely somewhere in the rainforest."

"The police said that her pilot sent a distress call but lost contact before they could give their coordinates," Dad said. "We have to wait and see. I know you're scared but the police will be looking for her. We'll have to leave it in their hands until I can get there."

We were all frightened. The police called every few hours at first but the calls became fewer and further between. Dad demanded answers but they hadn't discovered anything new. He made plans to fly to Manaus, the capital city of Amazonas in Brazil. That's where Mom was last seen. She flew there twice a year to work with other scientists in a lab at the local hospital. She did extensive research on the plant life in the Amazon Rainforest and discovered medicines that have been used in the hospitals in South America. Only this time, she hadn't come back.

The next day, our father left us behind to stay with our neighbors, Mr. and Mrs. Goldfarb. Sergio and I were fuming. Don't get me wrong. The Goldfarbs were a nice old couple, but we wanted to be in Brazil looking for Mom. Dad said it would be too dangerous and we'd be safer at home in

Northfork. We were anxious, and I paced a lot and had twisted my hair until I had a headache. Sergio was much more productive when he was anxious. He read a lot of books. This time he read about the Amazon and numerous versions of wilderness survival guides. It was like he was preparing for his own personal rescue mission.

Sergio was ten years old, three years younger than me, and had Dad's stocky build. He stood taller than most of the kids his age, so people assumed he was older. He was smart, a borderline genius, and loved everything there was to know about chemistry, astronomy, and biology. He was always engrossed in something he was reading or experimenting with.

My brother and I spent a lot of time together discussing the details of my dreams. Normally I would have found it somewhat annoying to have my little brother nosing around all of the time. But when he came to discuss my dreams, I didn't mind the intrusion. He was fascinated by the possibility to dream about future events. Once he tried to get me to predict the winning team for the Super Bowl but it just didn't work like that. I could never decide what I would dream about. Sometimes a dream was just a dream and nothing more. My brother helped me determine if it was simply a common dream or a premonition. He was very good at asking questions and gathering enough information to make a hypothesis.

I typically didn't remember my dreams but I know they were vivid. I was able to pick up on the faintest odors and hear the quietest of sounds. When all of my senses were affected, we knew that it was a premonition and they were sometimes tricky to interpret. They also could be quite obvious, like the time when I dreamed that I'd fallen from the Lawson's tree house. Luckily, I was able to talk everyone out of climbing that tree except for Joseph Lawson, who tried to prove that the tree branch was sturdy enough. He climbed and just before he reached the top, a branch broke and he fell. He wasn't hurt but he definitely had a bruised ego.

Other times, the dreams were not always obvious to me and I needed my brother's help. Sometimes he really surprised me. One morning, I dreamed of a stuffed bear tied down to railroad tracks. A train was coming down the tracks full force, heading directly for the bear. Denver Morgan, an angry loner, was driving the train.

I never thought about Mr. Morgan very much until that morning. But it was Sergio who figured out that it was likely that Mr. Morgan would be at the train station. He felt that the restrained teddy bear symbolized a child who would be threatened somehow. We agreed to go to the Northfork Train Station the next morning and watch from a distance. It turned out that Mr. Morgan was at the station, but the scenario wasn't as dire as we had thought. As the train arrived, a woman stepped out onto the platform holding the hand of a small boy. When Mr. Morgan noticed the child by her side, he turned and walked off towards his rusty old truck. We found out later from some teenagers in the neighborhood that Mr. Morgan had a daughter, Marlene, who he hadn't spoken to for eighteen years. I guess they planned to reconcile that day, but the bitter old man was unhappy to find out that he was now someone's grandfather.

When I tried to describe the event at the station to my parents, my father looked agitated. He said that we were looking for trouble and that I should have been a better role model for my little brother. Sergio found it insulting to be judged by his age. He'd probably make a better role model for someone my age than I would for someone his age. Since that time, I hadn't discussed my dreams with my dad. They were somewhat uneventful anyway until I began dreaming about my mother.

I spent the week feeling angry that our father had left us back home while our mother was lost somewhere in the largest rainforest in the world. Mostly we were just scared that they wouldn't return home at all. My brother and I tried to continue our daily routines. We went to school. We ate dinner with the Goldfarbs and had polite conversation. We even managed to joke around with friends. But we were just going through the motions.

When my father came back from Brazil, he looked exhausted. He had hired trackers to fly over villages in the Amazon where Mom had worked most. The police rummaged through every journal that my mother used and spoke to hotel managers and staff, along with numerous villagers along the coast of the Amazon River. But he had no luck. He came back home without Mom and with sadness in his eyes that I had never seen.

Sergio and I were glad to be sleeping in our own beds again. The Goldfarbs' house smelled of mothballs and their dog did not like our cat, Smokey, who had remained hidden under the bed most of the time. Still, they were kind and their food wasn't bad.

I woke up at some point in the middle of the night. My father heard me mumbling something and he came into my room. "Sorry. I didn't mean to wake you," I said.

"You didn't wake me. What's up?" he asked.

"I had another strange dream and I have to tell you about it before I forget," I began to ramble. "The air smelled very sweet… like sugar. I think it was the flowers."

"I never heard of flowers that smelled like sugar," Dad said. He gently brushed the hair away from my eyes and smiled. "Does sugar even have a smell?" he asked lightheartedly.

"No, I guess not. I just felt the smell came from the flowers."

"What else did you see?" Dad asked.

"I heard voices and…"

"And what?"

"You won't believe me." I lowered my eyes so that he wouldn't see my tears.

"Larissa, I'm listening. Tell me what you saw."

I paused for a few moments. "I heard Mom's voice. She was speaking to children, but not in English."

"Was it Portuguese?" he asked.

"No, I didn't recognize it. There was a painted boy… and he was sort of singing." I glanced up at my father who was squinting. I'd managed to lose some credibility. "Then I heard Mom's voice coming from my own mouth."

He pulled my fingers out of a tight loop in my disheveled curls and held my chin in his hand. He stared at me for a moment. I knew by the way he smiled that he was thinking how much I resembled my mother. We both had the same black curly hair, large, olive-colored eyes, and our frame was long and slender. Our mannerisms were similar and we walked as if books were balanced on our heads. Dad always said that we reminded him of two Persian cats. He sighed heavily. "Go back to sleep, Larissa. We'll talk more in the morning."

"Okay." I exaggerated a sigh and rolled over.

The next morning, I went into my father's study and saw maps of South America and his passport neatly bound with rubber bands on the edge of his desk. He had planned a second trip to Brazil. Sergio and I begged him to take us along but he told us that it would be too dangerous. We were both prepared to face whatever danger lay ahead because we knew how much we'd be needed.

"You know, Dad, I'm pretty observant. I've read books on forensic science and I'd probably find more leads in Manaus than the police have," Sergio said.

"You probably would," Dad said. He was making rice and beans and added too much garlic. The house smelled and my eyes burned.

"I've also read a lot about the Amazon. I'm well aware of the dangers. I also know about various foods we can make from the vines and the roots of plants."

"That's very useful," Dad said. He was fanning the smoke out towards the open window with a magazine.

"And most importantly, Larissa's dreams may lead us right to Mom," Sergio said. He smiled at me and gave an exaggerated wink.

"Uh huh. Sergio, can you pass me the garlic?" Dad asked.

He hadn't really been listening. Sergio and I glanced at each other and knew that we'd have to try again later. Mom did most of the cooking and it was probably best to let Dad concentrate before he burned down the kitchen.

After dinner, Sergio headed off to his room but before he left, he glanced in my direction, cocked his head to the right, and rolled his eyes in Dad's direction as if to say, "Keep pushing him." I waved him off silently.

My father and I cleaned the table in silence and piled the dishes in the sink. "So?" Dad sat down and ran his hands along the smooth, clean table. He reached for his cup and drank the last of his coffee. "Are we going to discuss the dreams?" Dad asked. His voice was soft. He tried to show me that he was going to listen this time and leaned forward with his chin in his hand, looking directly into my eyes. I was shrewder than he had thought. Nothing I said tonight would change his mind.

"No, it'll just make you mad."

"It's fine, Larissa. I promise I won't be mad."

We sat for an hour and discussed the dreams about the sugary-smelling flowers and the voices in the dark. I tried harder to remember the children I had seen, but it was difficult. It was like looking through a thick fog, one small detail at a time. "I remember two children and they had beautiful, elaborate drawings on their bodies. I don't know where Mom was, but I felt like she was standing there with me." Dad stared at the table, wide-eyed. He tried to be encouraging as I recalled the details of the dream, but I could see that he was just not convinced. I knew that I needed to prove myself... somehow.

Chapter 2

A Leap of Faith

The next morning, I made my father a pot of coffee. I always loved the smell, although my mother forbade me to drink it before I was in college. Instead, she made a breakfast shake that we drank each morning for as long as I could remember. I filled half of Dad's cup with coffee and the other half with hot milk typical in Brazilian culture. Sergio and I joined him at the table for breakfast. I decided to make pancakes. It was Dad's favorite and I thought it may put him in a better listening mood.

I waited for Dad to finish breakfast before I started the debate again. Smokey joined us at the table. Sergio attempted to clean the table and tried to reach above the stove into the cabinet where Mom kept the sugar. He loved to sprinkle some on his strawberries. He lost his balance and some sugar fell in the frying pan which was still hot from the pancakes. The aroma of browning sugar was familiar. "Wait! I remember something. I smelled the same thing in my dream. That was the sugary smell!" I said, leaping out of my chair and scaring the daylights out of my brother.

"Cooked sugar?" Dad asked.

"Yes, yes, it was like cotton candy! And I remember seeing a black bird or something with huge wings."

"A toucan?" Sergio asked.

"Yeah, I guess," I said, not really remembering.

"The children were dressed strangely. The boy wore red and blue beads around his neck, ankles, and wrists. He was dark-skinned and the front of his hair was shaved to the scalp. All he wore was a wrap around his waist. The girl wore a simple wrap around her as well, that covered most of her body except for her calves and arms. She also wore beads but only a single strand around both ankles. They spoke in a language that I couldn't understand. They seemed intelligent and showed me what to eat and what was poisonous. Then I realized that the girl was holding a hand that wasn't mine. I recognized the wedding band and the long fingers. I realized that it wasn't me that the boy was speaking to; it was Mom. I was seeing everything through Mom's eyes! The girl was holding *Mom's* hand!"

My father stared silently out the window. He didn't speak for a while. He finally gave us a sad look. Nothing I had said made him believe that my dreams were genuine.

"It's just wishful thinking, Larissa. I'm sorry, honey. I'll go back to Brazil next week but I'm going alone. It's just too dangerous to take you and your brother into the Amazon."

"Actually, many children live in the Amazon… What's two more?" Sergio said sarcastically. Dad laughed a little, which eased the tension. "Seriously, Dad, Larissa's dreams are real. I know firsthand. Even Mom believed her, so why can't you?" Sergio said.

"It's not that I don't believe you. It's that our dreams come from our subconscious minds and we cannot predict future events. The future is not determined. It hasn't occurred yet," Dad said.

There was really nothing more to say. I tried to sleep but I was jittery. My eyelids dropped slowly but they shot open again when I thought of Mom. I felt a lump in my throat. I must have finally gone to sleep because I woke to my father shaking me. I was confused and I was blinded by the light in my room.

"Larissa, what were you saying?" Dad asked.

"What? What… what did I say?"

"Where did you learn that?" he asked.

"I don't know what you mean. Learn what?"

"You were speaking another language. Who taught you that?" He gripped my shoulders firmly.

"Dad, I don't know…" I pried his fingers off my right arm. "Daaaad."

He lowered his hands. "Oh, sorry honey." This time he held my hand. "I'm just a little stunned. You were sitting up in bed. Your eyes were wide open and you were speaking to me for three minutes in some language. It was like… Portuguese, but it was a very old dialect that had not been spoken for centuries."

Sergio came in rubbing his eyes. He was listening through the walls. "You mean like Sanskrit?"

"Something like that," Dad said, nodding his head.

They were both staring at me now. I had no idea what had even happened. Dad and Sergio waited until I was able to gather my thoughts.

"It was Mom. She was speaking. I guess I was too. She was talking to that boy that I told you about. He spoke in the same language. It was like he was singing a song."

"It was beautiful," Dad said. He thought for a few moments.

"Dad, it's obvious that Larissa has more information than anyone else right now," Sergio said, breaking the silence.

Dad was thoughtful for a few seconds more. "That's it," he said, slapping his thigh. "I guess we're all taking a trip. We'll pack our bags tomorrow after school."

Sergio and I squealed. "We're going to get Mom!"

Dad left to make a phone call and I listened. "*Oi Ricardo.*" He spoke in Portuguese for a few minutes. I heard him say our names and the name of the hotel Mom had gone to numerous times before. He hung up the phone, sighed, and returned to my room.

"I spoke to Ricardo, your mother's assistant, who has kept in touch with the sergeant of the Manaus police. He explained that they could not send out a search party beyond the restricted borders of the Amazon. They have done all they can do."

"They can't keep explorers from traveling other regions of the Amazon for research," Sergio said.

"No, they can't. Any kind of research, documentation, and exploration can be done at the traveler's own risk. So he's contacted an old friend, José Vieira, who will lead our expedition. You must understand that this could be very dangerous for us all. When we reach Amazonas, I will discuss the plans further with Ricardo but we have to take many precautions. If you have any concerns about going, tell me now."

"Are you kidding? We're going, Dad."

I remember my mother telling me about Amazonas. It is the largest state in Brazil, even larger than Texas. It's covered in jungle with places that have never been explored. Mom had gone there many times to study the roots and plants for the lab. She often worked with one particular Amazonian tribe deep in the jungle. She never came back with any plant life or animal life because it was dangerous to our environment, so they did all the research in Brazil, which is why she went twice a year. She told me a story about a scientist who brought back a plant from the rainforest and planted it in his backyard. One day, the tree limbs began to shake as if it was going to jump right out of the ground. Thousands of spiders crawled out of the tree. They were social spiders, not poisonous, but they traveled and lived in large groups and would wreak havoc on the insect life in North America. They must have been in a cocoon and went unnoticed. Mom occasionally came back with some gifts and some spices for cooking but that was all she would bring.

"Okay, guys," Dad said. "We have a flight the night after next. Take only the necessities and get some sleep."

"We *will* find Mom," Sergio said. He sounded rather convincing.

"Let's hope so," Dad said.

I was hardly able to contain myself at school. Mr. Rush was watching me during the history exam because I kept staring out the window. I was excited to be going on an airplane, excited to be joining my father on an expedition, and most of all, excited to find Mom. There was no concrete evidence whatsoever that my mother was alive and in the Amazon, but my dreams and the feeling I had in my heart told me she was alive and needed our help. Mr. Rush tapped his pencil to get my attention. I tried to focus on my exam but knew I wasn't going to get my usual A- with a *Great Job* written in red.

After the bell rang at 2:45, I picked up Sergio at the elementary school. His principal was having a debate with his science teacher while Sergio was leafing through a pamphlet on school policies in the main office. Apparently, my little brother attempted to let the school snake loose in the garden, but instead it slithered back into the classroom while the science teacher was working with a group of students. I overheard the principal say that although things like this do happen, she was uncomfortable with the idea that a snake was loose in the building. She asked the teacher to gather some students who had stayed behind for the science club to search the grounds to find the snake. The science teacher nodded and quickly headed back to his classroom in search of Mr. Slithers, the harmless gardener snake. Meanwhile, the principal took a deep breath, straightened her suit, brushed off any lint, and headed directly towards Sergio.

"Sergio Ricci, may I see you in my office please?" the principal said in a stern voice.

Sergio looked at me, tightened his lips, and headed in, shuffling his feet along the way. I wasn't quite sure why he had walked that way until I heard a yelp behind the closed door. Of course I had to muffle my laugh because I was supposed to be the mature, older sister but I could only imagine the look on her face when my brother shocked her from the build-up of an electrical charge you can get while shuffling your feet across a carpet on a very dry, cold day.

He headed out of her office with a homework packet, a note for Dad, and a grin from ear to ear.

"You are in big trouble."

"It was worth it," Sergio said.

"Which part, letting the snake loose or frying the principal?"

"Both," Sergio said.

When we got home, Sergio explained his position while Dad carefully read and reread the principal's note. He explained that the snake incident was an accident. He was trying to return Mr. Slithers back to the cage but as he turned to search for the lid, the snake arched its back and slithered out. The teacher automatically assumed that he was trying to set the snake free but this was not the case.

"Amy Truehart set two white mice free last year and Mikey Polini set the frogs free the year before because he had just seen the movie ET where the kid, Elliot, had done the same," said Sergio.

"I'm more upset about the shock you gave the principal when you were in her office. That was uncalled for, Sergio."

"You're right. I shouldn't have done that," he whispered. "The science teacher just taught us about building an electrical charge and I was testing the theory. I really had no idea it would work. Believe me, Dad, I was as shocked as she was." Sergio looked at my father and giggled. "I'll write an apology note to the principal and I'll use my allowance to buy a new snake for the science room."

"Very wise. Let's not lose control again," Dad said.

We were both a little nervous that Dad would change his mind about our trip but that afternoon, he picked us both up and we headed directly to the airport. My brother and I were nervous and excited to board a 747 jet for the first time. The idea that we were traveling to South America, left me with goose bumps and sweaty palms. The airplane was huge with rows and rows of seats. Dad immediately took out his book on black holes and nestled in his seat. Sergio was already reading another survival guide for the rainforest, which kept him busy for hours. I read my teen magazines from cover to cover until I was absolutely sure that my favorite actors and actresses were all wearing what was in fashion for the month. I may not be able to dress like the stars but I certainly could keep up with the fashion trends. Mom had told me that Brazil is one step ahead in fashion compared to the United States. In other words, what's in today for North America was yesterday's trend for Brazil.

I didn't enjoy the plane's take-off, although I overheard the passengers behind me comment on how smooth it was. In spite of my nervousness, it was fascinating to see the objects on land getting smaller and smaller. The trees, the cars, and the buildings disappeared beneath the clouds until the sun set. I couldn't help being concerned that the pilots were unable to see in front of them in the dark, but Dad assured me that they use radar to determine where they are flying and how high the plane is compared to the ground as well as other objects. After dinner, which wasn't too bad by the way, we watched a James Bond movie and fell asleep. I slipped into a deep slumber and began to dream again.

The same beaded boy was pulling plants from the ground. He showed me the root of one plant and took a large bite. He didn't seem to mind the grit and I couldn't help laughing. I didn't recognize the plant but I took some anyway. When I looked down at my hand, I noticed the long, elegant fingers with a gold band and remembered that it was Mom with this young boy, not me. I felt closer to my mother more than ever now. I felt her hunger and her fatigue and wondered why she was out there alone without her assistants, or anyone else for that matter. I could hear whispering but I wasn't sure if it was part of the dream or from the people on the airplane.

Suddenly, I began running. I felt hot, tired, and hungry but mostly scared. A heavy weight forced my legs to buckle under and I ripped desperately at the plants on the round. The ground beneath me dropped and grew further and further away. I woke up with a gasp and a heavy weight on my shoulder. It was Sergio's head, and he was now snoring. I needed to talk to him and nudged him softly. He was a deep sleeper, so I shook my shoulders which caused his head to bounce. No luck. Finally, I reached up to air-conditioning jets and aimed them directly toward my brother's head. He woke gasping from the cold burst of air.

"You're mean," he said.

"Sorry but I have to talk to you. I had another dream."

"Save it for someone who's interested."

"I'll let you have my peanuts."

He thought for a moment. "Throw in the pretzels and we've got a deal."

I tossed him the miniature-sized food bags. Sergio's maniacal laugh reminded me of an old movie. I explained in detail what I had seen. I described how Mom's hands clutched at the plants.

"Maybe she was being dragged by her feet," said Sergio. "Maybe something was chasing her, caught her, threw her down, and dragged her back to his village to eat her."

"This is our mother you are talking about!"

"Sorry." He thought for a moment. "Did you see the ground and plants moving away from you or towards you?" asked Sergio. "You may have been falling, you know."

"Away from me. I remember her fingernails being dragged in the dirt. I also remember the native boy who appeared to get farther and farther away."

We both grew quiet. I knew that Mom was in danger. I wished I could help her but I just didn't have enough information to be helpful.

"Was she screaming?" he asked.

Was she? "Wait, she was not screaming. She was scared but didn't shout out once. In fact, the boy she was with looked terrified but he didn't make a sound. Why would Mom not scream for help if she was being attacked?"

Suddenly the plane began shaking. Our drinks toppled over and a man stretching his legs in the aisle began to fall towards the center row of passengers. He was caught by another man who was still buckled in. A woman in the back let out a shriek, a child cried, and I gasped along with a few others. Dad woke up and threw open the window shade. I closed my eyes and held my breath until the plane stopped shaking and we were steady.

The pilot came on the speaker and said, "Ladies and gentlemen, please remain in your seats with your seatbelts fastened."

The flight attendants walked briskly to their own seats. Dad always told us that he would look at the faces of the flight attendants to see if we were in any danger. I guess they would look worried if something was truly wrong. They didn't look worried but they did exactly what the pilot said.

Dad whispered into Sergio's ear. My brother nodded and closed his eyes as if he were falling asleep.

"Are you going to tell me what Dad said?"

"It's gonna cost you."

"Alright, here's my apple."

Sergio laughed. "Sucker. It's just a little turbulence."

The pilot's voice came over the speaker. "It's alright, folks, just some turbulence. We'll fly a little higher and try to avoid it for a smoother flight."

I snatched back my apple and stretched my neck to see out the tiny window. Lush green trees filled the land as far as the eye could see. I could tell we were landing any minute, so I clutched the armrests until my knuckles turned white.

The passengers seemed relieved as the plane touched down on the runway. I stepped off the plane and felt the warm breeze. My legs were wobbly as I climbed down the steps and looked back to see the massive contraption that flew thousands of miles. It was all so unnatural.

"Amazing, isn't it?" Dad said.

Sergio nodded. "Ah yes, Brazil, the melting pot of the world, including the largest rainforest which contains more than half of the ten million species of animals, plants, and insects in what is known as the Amazon Rainforest," Sergio said as he continued to recite his South American travel books in which he had been completely absorbed. My brother was amazing. If you gave him a book, he'd memorize every fact in a day. If you gave him a book that didn't interest him, he'd barely remember its shape.

We grabbed our luggage and Dad saw Mom's assistant, José, waiting for us with his jeep. Dad and José hugged tightly. José offered kind words and said he was still hopeful. We climbed into the jeep and he took us to our hotel in Manaus. We were all very tired from travel. I didn't know how Mom and Dad traveled like this so often, but I was happy to be standing on solid ground.

As we drove away, I watched the planes take off overhead. It seemed strangely familiar. Suddenly it hit me. I realized that Mom hadn't been dragged on the ground. She had been lifted off the ground. She had been lifted up towards the treetops as the boy watched in horror. I decided to wait to tell my father and Sergio. José wouldn't have understood and would think Dad was crazy for entertaining the entire idea.

Chapter 3

The Expedition

We checked into the hotel and had dinner with José. Two more men joined us who, as Dad explained, were excellent pilots. The men spoke in Portuguese. My father did too, and it frustrated me. Sergio and I wanted to know what the plans were but we kept quiet. We pretended to keep busy eating, playing with our food, and folding the linen napkins into fans but we were really listening for any words that sounded familiar. They spoke too fast and I couldn't decipher one word from the next. Sergio looked uncomfortable but I felt suddenly at ease because we all had the same objective: to find Mom.

After dinner, we went back to our rooms. Dad had to practically carry Sergio, who was exhausted. The elevator lifted off the ground with a jolt and instantly brought me back to my dream. I felt a similar feeling when Mom got yanked from her crouching position. It was unsettling.

"Larissa, since when are you afraid of elevators?" Dad asked.

"I'm not. I had another dream about Mom and..." I began talking a mile a minute about the dream sequence. Even Sergio perked up to hear my newest discovery of

Mom being airlifted from the ground. Dad looked puzzled and a little suspicious. I began to worry about him losing faith in me now.

"It was real, Dad. I know it sounds crazy, but Mom was lifted off the ground by something. She didn't scream or anything. It doesn't seem realistic but I felt it. It was happening to Mom but I felt everything and saw everything through her eyes. I felt my feet leave the ground and I was being pulled upward."

"Then why do you suppose she didn't scream?" Dad asked. "Mom screams when she sees a smudge on the new wallpaper. Why not from this?"

"I don't know. Maybe she was too scared to scream." The elevator doors opened. It was late, so no one spoke any further until we reached the room. Sergio collapsed on the bed while I brushed the knots from my hair.

My father looked out the window of our room for some time. "We have a very long day ahead of us tomorrow, so let's hit the hay. We'll discuss this more in the morning."

I heard my father tossing and turning in bed all night. I hated to worry him but he needed to know the facts. I woke up to the phone ringing. It was 5:00 A.M. and José was calling the room so we could meet for breakfast and get an early start.

After breakfast, we headed off to the prop plane. It was a small yellow contraption that held only six people. It had propellers which were very loud and made the whole plane vibrate when José started it up. The plane coasted down the runway, sending my stomach up into my throat. I couldn't breathe as the plane took off. I had to imagine my body catching up to its speed. I started to feel better until José dipped the wings left and then right. I just prayed that he wouldn't take a sudden nosedive to impress us. Of course, he did. I was not impressed. I was pretty sure my face had turned green and wished I hadn't eaten breakfast. Sergio squealed and my father remained silent.

Within minutes, we reached the Amazon Rainforest and saw miles and miles of treetops and not much more. The colors were vivid. The trees were rich with vibrant shades of green. The sun's glow peeked up over the horizon and created an orange streak across the sky. The plane weaved back and forth and we stretched our necks to see out the windows to search the forest for anything unusual.

"It will be very difficult to find the crash site," José said. "There will no longer be fire or smoke. It has been too long." José's accent was thick and he yelled over the noisy propellers but I was able to detect the solemn tone to his voice.

"What if the plane didn't crash? What if it somehow landed in a clearing?" Dad asked.

"It's unlikely. The excavations are not completely cleared out and the tree stumps remain, so it would be very dangerous to land. She did not take a water plane, so she could not land in the Anavilhanas River," José said.

"Why did she take a prop plane? She usually traveled by boat," Dad said.

"This was the first time she requested a plane. She typically didn't travel that deep into the forest. Your wife's work never took her more than ten miles inward and forty miles along the Amazon River because the plants and roots are easily found by the water's edge. That day, her pilot called into the tower. He informed the men on duty that they would be flying westward. She had been studying an exotic plant found near the Xingavi tribe. Now, many of the tribes are being forced out of their homes due to deforestation and have moved into areas that are dangerous and unexplored. She must have learned that the Xingavi tribe moved as well."

"Could she have flown towards the center of the rainforest instead of along the water's edge?" Dad yelled.

"It's a possibility. We only assumed it was because of the tribe's new location. On Sunday morning, she headed out and never returned. The logbook states the time and the coordinates but they were not found anywhere along that route. They must have changed course."

"But if she knew she couldn't land the plane, why would she fly?" asked Dad.

José said, "Her journal notes mentioned that they were running out of time. She was desperate to find the tribe, get the plants, and get back to the lab. She must have been onto something. Perhaps she planned to take a boat after she spotted the location of the village. I don't believe that she had any intention of landing out there."

"How did she know where to find the new village?"

"Dione is very special, Luca. She always found what she was looking for by instinct alone. She scared the men with her wit and knowledge."

"Then what are you waiting for? Head into the Amazon!" Dad said eagerly.

"Yes, but when the gas tank is half empty, we're going to head back," José said cautiously.

We traveled for quite some time. As green as I was feeling, I didn't want José to head back to the hangar. I felt closer to my mother more than ever and did not want one more day to go by without seeing her face. José and my father were discussing other options. They mentioned something about heading back to Manaus and chartering a boat. I just had this feeling in the pit of my stomach that one more day could be disastrous.

Suddenly, José dipped the wing and began to turn the plane around. We all grew quiet and reserved. None of us wanted to stop looking but it was too dangerous to keep going with a gas tank that was half-empty. Sergio had fallen asleep at some point and I realized that my eyes were getting heavy as well. I closed my eyes while bright lights flashed over and over inside my eyelids. Memories of dense foliage, a tranquil stream, and the sun setting, reflecting its light on the trunks of trees, all formed in my mind. Attached to each trunk was a red tag. My eyes shot open and I shook my brother's shoulder, causing his head to bobble.

"Hey, cut it out," Sergio said. He sounded annoyed and closed his eyes again. I whispered what I had remembered from my dreams and he flipped open his Amazonian ecology book. It contained photographs of trees that were tagged for loggers to cut down. I recognized the red tags.

"Where will the next excavation take place?" Sergio asked.

"They will begin to cut south of Coari," José said.

"When?" Sergio asked.

"They start tomorrow morning." José looked confused and the two men turned their heads to get a better look at Sergio. They were all baffled by his questions.

"Dad, we have to go south of Coari."

"Why? What's going on, Sergio?" Dad asked. He didn't answer. "Larissa?"

"I don't know." I looked at him wide-eyed. "We just do." I glanced over toward José and back to my father. José glanced at the men and then at my father, waiting for an explanation. My eyes opened wider but I was silent.

My father had understood. "We need to head to Coari, amigos. From there, we will head south toward the excavation. We'll go by boat tomorrow."

My father didn't get into a detailed explanation with José or the trackers. His instructions to travel westward must have seemed odd, especially because they would be heading towards the excavation site. Nevertheless, they followed their instructions as my father had discussed with José.

When we got back to the hotel, the men sat at a separate table and quietly discussed the plan to charter a boat. They spoke in English this time and I, of course, could hear every word. My hearing had gotten better since we'd reached Brazil. Sergio was intrigued by this and kept asking me what the men were saying. I often wondered why I have *poderes* and why Sergio did not. My mother had once mentioned in private that she too had *poderes*. She said she hadn't used it in so long and had probably lost her abilities. Sergio had no idea. He had expectations that he'd gain *poderes* as well, but my mother felt he should be focused on studies and more important things. I can't think of anything that is more important than my premonitions. In fact, without them, I'd be home in Northfork right now, worrying about both of my parents.

Dad asked for two Zodiacs to navigate the smaller rivers, a week's worth of gasoline, and a first-aid kit with anti-venom serums and penicillin. The men discussed the dangers that we all were facing, and the treacherous journey, and then they began to speak in Portuguese. Dad looked irritated. He said, "Good night," tipped the waiter, and gathered his papers and maps. "Let's go to bed. We have a big day ahead of us."

I was a little worried that I misinterpreted the dream on the prop plane. Maybe I dreamed of the red tags because I had seen it in one of Sergio's books. My father had begun to take my dreams seriously now, which was a lot of pressure for a kid. I was happy that he trusted me and I couldn't risk making a single mistake.

"You kids need to pack your hats, long-sleeve shirts, undergarments, and toothbrushes. That's all you'll need. Anything more will feel like fifty pounds and we will be hiking for many miles each day. I want you to be comfortable. Are you sure you're up for it?" Dad asked. We both nodded.

"Larissa, wake me if you have any dreams tonight. It's very important that you share every detail," my father said, yawning. He stretched out his arms and appeared to me as a giant.

"Alright, Dad." I hugged him tight, partially because I was afraid, but mostly because he believed in me. "Good night." I felt the exhaustion run down my arms and legs as I settled back onto my pillow. Even my head felt tired. My eyelids closed and I dreamed throughout the night. I woke every few hours and wrote down as many details as possible. My father and Sergio continued to sleep and it was just as well. There was no sense keeping them up. I scribbled for half the night and slept hard until morning. I woke and found my brother flipping through pages in my journal. "Hey! What are you doing?"

"Just curious. So… you had a dream that you were flying?" Sergio asked.

"Not me. Mom was flying." I yanked the journal out of his hands and began to twist my hair. I had to stop this annoying habit. My hair was a mess.

"But you wrote, 'I am flying through the air.' You underlined the word *I* three times and you wrote, 'Mom flew through the air,' in the entries written yesterday. Anyway, no biggie, we all have dreams that we fly once in a while," he said.

I rubbed my eyes some more and yawned. "Yeah, I guess. I must have been pretty tired."

"I don't understand why I keep having the same dreams over and over. I see Mom pulling at roots and plants and suddenly she gets lifted from the ground. Except each time it happens, I see a different view of the ground and the children as I am lifted. No one screamed. No one moved. They just watched Mom fly off. They looked terrified."

"It's my guess that your mother knew what she was doing," Dad said. He was dressing and had missed a button, making his shirt crooked and unkempt. He suddenly appeared to me as a child.

"What do you mean? She wanted to get abducted? That doesn't sound logical," Sergio said.

He began unbuttoning his shirt and started again. "Your mother said she had *poderes* at one time. Her instincts were very sharp. She was always sure about something based on her own intuitiveness. I used to tease her and said she just had excellent guessing capabilities but she knew that it was something much more substantial. It was strange how she knew that you fell that time in school, Sergio, and called the nurse before she could call us. She also sensed something was going to happen at Joseph Lawson's house. That day, your mother made sure Mr. Lawson would be home by calling him for some gardening tips. Sure enough, Joseph fell from the tree house. She hadn't known, however, about Mr. Morgan's train station adventure and was really mad at herself for not sensing the danger."

"But there was no real danger," I said.

"Yes, but your mother would have sensed the *possibility* of danger at one time. I think she realized that her instincts were getting rusty. She said that it was probably because she hadn't really displayed her true *poderes* since she was a child. But she had to stop using it. At that time, people didn't understand, especially in a quiet town."

"What would they have done, burned her at the stake and called her a witch?" Sergio said lightheartedly.

"No. She would have been institutionalized. People fear the unknown. Your mother had to be very careful not to draw attention to herself."

"So she planned the abduction? Why would she do that?" I asked.

"If her instincts were even slightly functional, Mom would have sensed danger and would have hidden before she could be grabbed," Dad said. "So she must have let it happen."

"So why do you think she didn't scream?"

"She was protecting the children," Sergio said. "Maybe screaming would have scared them."

"Maybe," Dad said. "It still seems awfully risky. It's unlikely your mother would put her own life in jeopardy unless it was to save the lives of others." We all feared this was exactly what had happened. The room was silent as we finished getting ready.

We made our way to the dock at 6:00 A.M. to find José and the men waiting. We boarded the fishing boat, which was large and flat without sides. There was just a cabin to keep the rain off our heads. There were nets and rods set up with buckets of smelly fish guts called chum. Colorful hooks and lures were displayed in a box with rubber worms and other strange metallic things that would entice hungry fish. The cabin smelled musty and looked weathered. There were fish remains on a countertop from fillets recently cut. A mesh bag containing lemons hung from a hook. The men loaded the supplies and attached the two Zodiacs which were small boats made of a tough black rubber with a small motor. Dad untied the ropes from the dock and pushed the boat hard with his foot to move it away, but he was still able to leap onto the deck. José casually saluted the two men and we pushed off down the river.

"It has no sides," squealed Sergio. "Cool!"

A boat with no sides is an adventure for a precocious and devious little kid. As the boat drifted down the river, the two men jumped into their jeep and took off.

"Where are the pilots going, Dad? Aren't they coming with us?"

"No, they'll be flying toward Coari," Dad said as he browsed through my journal. "They'll radio in if they see anything unusual. Now what's this about the black bats?"

"Black bats?" I hesitated. "I don't... oh yeah, I remember. There were gigantic black bats." I shivered. "They made high-pitched squealing sounds and had wings that looked like giant hands. It's coming back to me now."

"Chiroptera," Sergio said. "It comes from the Greek words *cheir*, meaning hand and *pteron,* meaning wing."

"What else?" Dad asked.

"That's all I can think of, but I'll let you know if I can remember anything else."

Sergio looked impatient but Dad understood. He knew that I was feeling a lot of pressure and that they were relying solely on me and my dreams to find Mom.

As we sailed down the black river, I took note of the environment, the sounds, and the scent in the air. I hoped that something would feel familiar. The beautiful birds cawed up in the canopies and squirrel monkeys swung in the understory from limb to limb, screeching and hooting. They looked curiously at us while one monkey kept pace with the speed of our boat. Eventually it stopped cold and dangled from a vine, finally turning back. It was hot and damp but I liked the sun warm on my face and the sound of the trees rustling from the gentle breeze. All of it was incredible, but not familiar.

After we had sailed for two hours or so, the men signaled Dad and José by radio. It was difficult to hear them over the static and they had to keep asking the men to repeat themselves. As the men spoke back and forth, my brother and I waited for a sign on Dad's face that they had seen something by plane.

"They spotted the wing of a plane in the canopies ten miles east of Coari. They're going to pass by again to see if they can see the identification number," Dad said.

We all sat quietly, holding our breath until the men signaled again. It felt like an hour had passed and when they signaled back, Dad and José smiled and shook hands. They found Mom's plane. We had mixed emotions. Although we were happy to find the location of Mom's plane, no one had known if she was alright. José took out his map and they discussed how we were to travel for five days to reach Coari and we would stop only for resources when in need.

The sun had nearly set. A soft glow peeked through the trees on the hidden horizon. Dad and José fished while Sergio looked through my entries in the journal.

"I've been thinking," Sergio said. "I'll bet I know why you have the same dream over and over again."

"Why?"

"If you can see Mom's point of view, it's possible you're seeing it through the point of view of others. Mom's pilot may have been abducted. Maybe some of the Indians were too," Sergio said.

I must have looked confused, so he continued.

"Well, everyone sees the world a little bit differently. You're probably seeing everything from the eyes of each victim. They were all taken the same way." He bit into his mango and its juice dripped down his face.

I thought about this for a while. "That's why each time I saw a different view of the ground, of different faces looking up at me. I remember seeing other children. They were running."

"If you're right, there are a lot of people in danger," he said.

"We're going to need an army," I said.

"So, what's your gut feeling about Mom?" Sergio looked up with unblinking eyes. This was a question that I couldn't answer. I didn't have my mother's intuitiveness and I wasn't even sure how accurate my dreams were because nothing had been proven. "Do you think she's okay?"

"My gut feeling?" Sergio stared down into the black water. I put my arm around him and hugged him tight.

"She's alive."

Chapter 4

Lost

We continued down the river, passing fishing boats along the way, with people hard at work. It was the world's second longest and widest river. Two days felt like two years. We were entertained by the rose-colored dolphins that leaped in and out of the river. They traveled together in a pod, always crossing in front of the boat playfully. They seemed happy and carefree. It lightened the mood and passed the time.

José described the life of each animal we had encountered, its predators and prey, and its social behaviors. My brother, the human encyclopedia, always had his input. Sergio spent hours reading about plants, mammals, insects, and fish, and then spewed out bits of information each day as it barely related to the situation. For example, I had been eating a mushroom burger two weeks before. Sergio found that particular moment to discuss fungus and its tendency to grow in 'animal excrement.' I knew what he had meant but I didn't stop eating. I tried not to let him get the best of me. Besides, the burger was great.

We saw a troop of howler monkeys. Sergio explained how the saggy chin of this species acts as a resonating chamber. This is why they were able to make such loud, howling sounds. They could be heard for several miles so that one group was able to communicate with another. They did this to protect their homes and their families. I imagined how it would sound if every human communicated the same way. I realized that I was lucky to be able to communicate with my mother; even if it were through future events, I was seeing her and experiencing her world.

In the evenings, while Dad and José fished, Sergio swam in a channel where the river flow was calm and safe. The water looked dark and questionable and I stayed on the boat.

"I don't swim with piranha."

"Piranha will only attack when they smell blood," Sergio said, laughing.

"Thanks, I'll pass."

"C'mon, Larissa, stop being a big baby," Sergio said. He had begun to annoy me.

Suddenly, Sergio opened his eyes, let out a yelp, and sank under the water. I laughed at first but he was under for quite a while and I had begun to panic. I shifted glances at Dad and José, then back at the water, and back at Dad. I gasped when Sergio's air bubbles stopped floating to the surface. Dad glanced at me. While he was in the middle of a conversation with José, he walked to the stern of the boat and reached his hand into the water, pulling Sergio up by his hair, without missing a beat.

"Stop scaring your sister," Dad said sternly and continued to the bow of the boat. Sergio had a huge grin on his face. He climbed out of the water and looked quite proud of his accomplishment.

After dinner, the boat started up and Sergio and I unraveled the ropes from a tree where it had been tied. We jumped on board as my father had done the first day. I was getting used to the movement of the boat, strategically shifting my feet to avoid wobbling.

I understood why my parents loved it here. I had seen the greenest jungle ever imagined, and at night, the moon's reflection was cast on the river and had created just enough light to reflect the eyes of curious animals peering at our boat. It was their time to hunt, eat, and explore.

Dad and José took turns driving while the others slept. We were to reach Coari sometime the next day. "Get plenty of rest. It's going to be a long journey by Zodiac and then by foot," Dad said.

The next morning, José and my father were mapping the coordinates of my mother's plane. "These coordinates are way off course, Luca. Dione's plane should not have been that far out. The Xingavi tribe couldn't have traveled to Coari that quickly. It would have taken them months."

"Did the pilot miscalculate?" Dad asked.

"Her pilot was an excellent aviator. It was no mistake. No tribe would ever move that deep into the Amazon that fast. It's unlikely for any tribe to travel so deep. It's just too dangerous and too far from water. But still, they wouldn't have flown out that far accidentally."

"It does seem strange," Dad said.

I was suspicious about Mom's intentions. She was friendly with the tribesmen. They had taught her how to find roots found deep in the ground and grind them up with other exotic plants. She had found cures for illnesses with the knowledge they'd shared. Then why was she so off course?

Was she looking for the Xingavi tribe or was there something else?

We reached our destination by noon and we unhooked the Zodiacs. José pulled them off into the water and we began to load the cargo. We took only the necessities. José took a walkie-talkie, a box with a pot, pan, knife, spatula, matches, and flashlights. My father took a fishing rod with some hooks, the other walkie-talkie, mosquito netting, machete, and a tarp. Sergio had his olive-green backpack with change of clothes, beef jerky, a Swiss army knife, and his survival guides. I squeezed my clothes, hairbrush, toothbrush, teen magazine, lip gloss, and journal into my metallic silver backpack. José took one Zodiac while the rest of us climbed into the other. We sped through the channels which became so narrow that we pushed leaves and vines from our faces and ducked under low branches. We hadn't bothered with insect-repellent because it never seemed to repel anything. Dad explained that mosquitoes were attracted to carbon dioxide and we would just have to deal with it so long as we plan to breathe.

We traveled for about three hours and stopped by a village to rest. The houses in the village were on stilts, high above the ground. The roofs were thatched, completely made from the trees and bamboo. The dwellings were simple, just one large room where each family slept. My father told us that the villagers were called Caboclos, descendants of Indians and settlers. They ate together around a fire pit where they laughed, told stories, and children played. They were poor, simple farmers and fishermen, but they knew more about the animals and plants of the forest than anyone else.

It was a completely different life from ours. It made me appreciate the closeness of family and friends and I missed my home life. I loved the way Mom, Dad, Sergio, and I would sit in front of the fireplace in the winter months and we'd laugh as our marshmallows would fall from the skewers during our attempt to make s'mores. I missed Mom's laugh and the way her face would twist and wrinkle when she was grossed out by the marshmallow mess. I missed the way Dad would sweep Mom's hair from her face when she tried to eat the gooey, lopsided sandwich and the way Sergio looked with it all over his face. I missed my friends, my room, my… well, not school but I definitely miss Harry James. He was the boy I sat next to in English that always knew how to make me laugh.

The channel split and Dad and José agreed to separate while staying in contact by walkie-talkie. Dad, Sergio, and I traveled for a few hours when Sergio looked up towards the sun, studied its position, and scratched his chin. "Looks like it's around 4:30, Dad," Sergio said.

"Yep, we'd better stop to eat. We have to hike on foot soon and we need our strength."

Dad radioed José, but no one answered. He tried over and over to make contact but got no reception. I was getting a little nervous and had taken for granted how important José was to the expedition. Dad was great at reading maps, so I gave myself permission to relax. He had wilderness-survival experience from yearly trips through the Amazon and had extensive knowledge about plant life for his research. But we all knew just how dangerous it could be out here even for the most skilled tracker. Mom once told me a story about a group of men, five photographers, who traveled through some unexplored parts of the Amazon to take pictures of the wildlife for their magazines. Only one man made it out alive, starving, with some infected mosquito bites and broken ribs from falling while running from an anaconda. Expert or novice, the Amazon is unpredictable and dangerous.

We ate some dried fruits and meats until we felt satisfied. Dad handed us camu-camu fruits, small round fruits that were tart, crunchy, and full of vitamins. I was reluctant to eat anything that I had not sampled before but we were all so hungry. It was actually delicious. We pushed off again and Dad continued to call José but still there was no answer.

"Where did he go? Did he leave the boat?" My voice trembled with a heightened pitch. "Do you think something happened to him?"

"Calm down, Larissa. José knows this rainforest better than anyone and will be fine," Dad said, but he sounded unconvincing.

We headed towards a lagoon and dragged the boat up onto the sand. We put on our backpacks and headed towards the jungle.

"Now listen to me very carefully. It can be very dangerous. Remember what I told you," Dad said.

Sergio began to rattle off Dad's instructions verbatim. "Never jump over a fallen tree. Always climb up on top and look over for snakes on the other side. Don't walk through tall grass without looking down. Don't stick your hands in dark places. Don't eat anything unless we're positive of what plant it is. Don't pick up any animals unless you are absolutely positive they are not poisonous."

"Scratch that. Don't pick up any animal, period," Dad said.

We nodded and began to walk. Dad stopped short just before the dense jungle and said, "If anything happens to me, use the walkie-talkie and get help. These are our coordinates and we're heading west. Take my compass and head east to the boat. You'll be safe in the lagoon."

We nodded again. I had a knot in my stomach and a lump in my throat. We stepped into the deep green jungle. The aroma of moss and wet leaves filled the air. We walked single file as Dad bushwhacked his way through the dense foliage. I was impressed by the way he used his machete, swinging his arm downward and slicing through the thick branches and leaves. He told us that his father gave the machete to him when he was just twelve years old and taught him how to do everything from bushwhacking to filleting catfish. Grandpa was a great archeologist who traveled through the deserts of Egypt and the mountains of the Himalayas in search of tombs and historical artifacts. He learned to survive in all kinds of dangerous climates and weather conditions. He taught Dad everything he knew, but died before I was born.

My mother's father was a Caboclo. He fished before sunrise; the best time to fish when it wasn't so hot. Then he would farm before the afternoon. When it cooled off, just before dusk, he would explore the floor of the rainforest. He pulled plants that had medicinal properties for the local scientists. They paid him in exchange for the grueling work. He was very knowledgeable and became the most sought after farmer in the Amazon. That's how my parents became scientists, by the influence of their fathers.

All afternoon and evening, we followed Dad through the jungle. We suffered from a few insect bites and a minor snake scare but it was only a loose vine that dropped down onto my head. Sergio couldn't get enough of the redeye tree frogs that perched on the limbs of the twisted trees and he would jot a few things down in his journal occasionally which was threaded by a thin vine and tied like a necklace around his neck. We were all very tired and drenched in sweat. It was a slow walk through the dense parts and easier through the clearings. Suddenly, Dad stopped short. I wasn't watching where I was walking and crashed into him. Sergio giggled.

"What's wrong?" I asked.

My father was silent. The trees had all been cut down and for miles there were stumps left behind. It was silent now. Not a single bird chirped nor any monkey howled. My father crouched down and ran his hand along the stump of what was once a huge tree. Sergio picked up a red tag that had fallen. We reached the tagging area but there was no longer a single tree left, just an empty field of stumps. I felt like I had just stepped onto a graveyard. It was a sight you never get used to. We walked to the edge of the clearing before the rainforest was dense and whole again.

"It's getting dark. We're camping here tonight," Dad said.

We laid out the tarp and crawled on top. Dad made a fire and we ate more dried foods. I was determined to put up a tent and pounded stakes into the ground using a rock. I hung the mosquito netting over a tree limb and wrapped the ropes from the corners of the net around each stake. It was not much but it gave me a sense of protection from the jungle and I was satisfied with my attempt.

"Great tent, Larissa," Dad said. He looked very impressed.

"Not bad for a girl," Sergio said.

"Not bad for a genius," I said with pride.

"Okay genius, what do we do if it rains?" Sergio asked. I was annoyed by his mocking tone.

"Uh, I hear the weather will be warm and breezy tonight." I hadn't a clue what the weather would be like but I was embarrassed that my mosquito net roof might not have been the wisest choice.

That night, the rain came down hard while Sergio giggled his way through dinner. Luckily, Dad could tell that it would rain and rearranged the tarp and the mosquito netting so that we stayed dry and free of creepy bugs.

Dad cut down and prepared some edible plants he had found in the jungle. The pataua palm fruits were dark purple, about the size of an olive, and were delicious. He prepared an interesting tea made from the una de gato vine. While we ate, he told us about a Greek legend of a group of warriors called Amazon Women. I was fascinated, and although it was only a legend, I imagined strong, courageous women fending for themselves and taking on their enemies with bows and arrows. Stories like these always gave me a bit of inspiration.

I tuned in and out of my brother's debate with Dad while I read my magazines by firelight. They discussed everything from politics to religion. This time I was more attuned to the subject as I was there in the very rainforest they were discussing.

"Why don't people get how important the Amazon is to the ecological system? I mean, all of this could be completely destroyed within forty to fifty years? It could be completely wiped out in seventy-five to hundred years!" Sergio said.

"I think people are beginning to realize this and some are actually doing some things to stop deforestation. But people are stubborn. Politicians, large companies, even science has their hand in this," Dad said.

"It says right here that more than twenty percent of the world's oxygen is produced in the Amazon, and the thousands of animal species and the medicines produced from the plants are all being wiped out." Sergio tapped the pages in his ecology book. "What do they think the Earth will be like fifty years from now if they keep this up?" Sergio looked around at the hundreds of tree stumps. We all looked.

"I don't know what they think. Some people probably feel that it will be someone else's problem. Fortunately, not everyone thinks that way," Dad said, smiling at both of us.

I drifted off to sleep. Their voices echoed in and out of my ears. I dreamed again. It lasted what seemed like hours. I dreamed that the jungle was on fire. Sergio and I were under water and could see up towards the flames. I saw the bats again, flying over the water in the night sky while I was pulled under deeper and deeper until everything was black. I could still feel Sergio's hand but could also feel someone else's hand. It was small, like a child's hand, and I was comforted.

Chapter 5

The Villagers

That evening, I woke up to my father hollering in pain. Sergio and I jumped up and made our way out of the tent to look for Dad. We ran towards his cries in the dark night. Sergio grabbed my hand and led me through the blackness. He walked with speed and confidence. I was so scared. I couldn't see my own hand in front of my face. I just closed my eyes in fear of slamming into something. We walked quickly and Sergio led me around trees, stumps, and marshy waters. We were barely able to see our father lying on the ground. He was alert and struggling to stand. I began to call him but Sergio put his hand on my mouth, muffling my voice. We reached for our father to help him up and he cried out. His leg was twisted, probably broken, and although I could hardly see, I could tell by his rigid arms and closed fists that he was in a good deal of pain.

"Run! Run!" Dad screamed.

"Dad!" My mouth was covered again, and I was pulled away from my father.

The moon appeared from behind the clouded sky for only a moment, enough to see a giant bat yanking my father up by his shoulders, and before I could blink into the sky beyond my reach. I was paralyzed. I could see Sergio looking upward but he was completely silent. That was when I realized that it wasn't Sergio's hand covering my mouth. I tried to scream but the hand closed tighter and my brother ran to help muffle my cries. Sergio whispered, "It's alright, Larissa. He's here to help us."

I quickly turned with tears streaming from my eyes and had expected to see José. Instead, it was a young boy, an Amazonian child. His eyes looked deeply into mine and he motioned to stay silent. Sergio seemed to understand everything that had happened, and although the boy hadn't said a word, my brother knew we needed to remain completely silent or the bat would be back. I was shaking like a leaf and was too petrified to move. I hoped this was just a dream and the bat would bring my father safely back to us, but I knew from the feeling in the pit of my stomach that it wouldn't.

The boy led us through the forest on a journey that felt like hours. We walked in silence. I felt lost and helpless and surrendered to my brother and this stranger as they led me through the forest. I hadn't a clue where I was being led. The clouds must have dissipated because the moon was bright.

Now that I could finally see, I studied the boy. He must have been around my age – thirteen, maybe fourteen. He wore red and blue beads around his ankles and wrists. He was the boy I had dreamed about. I felt as if I had already known him. We rested on a rock by the edge of a small pond with a tiny waterfall. He offered us food that I had never eaten and found it to be sweet and salty at the same time. Sergio and I were exhausted and were breathing hard but the boy seemed completely rested. The front of his head had been shaven in a crescent shape and had a long and very thin braid down the back. He had a beautiful tattoo around his right eye, which continued down his neck and over his right shoulder. The design was completely in black and as I looked closer, I realized it was a single line that weaved inward and out, becoming bursts of elaborate spirals that unwound back into a single line. He was clothed in a simple wrap made from an animal skin but looked thin and smooth like expensive leather. He had a calming effect on us both and I felt safe with him.

"His name is Tavi," Sergio said.

I snapped, "How do you know this? He hasn't spoken. *We* haven't spoken in hours! How did you find your way to Dad in the dark? Why didn't you scream when Dad was taken by that… that freakishly large bat! What's going on, Sergio?" I was out of control now. I was crying and getting louder. Sergio and Tavi stood up quickly and grabbed both of my arms. A shriek came from the treetops, and before I could look up, I was being pulled toward the pond.

"Take a deep breath and hold it," Sergio said.

I did as the boys said, and we all dove into the pond. Well, *they* dove and yanked me in with them. We swam towards the waterfall, took one more deep breath, and we dove under the rocks and followed Tavi through a cave. I was able to see daylight through the opening on the other side of the cave. I was thankful that we took swimming lessons at such an early age, as one never knows if they'll wind up in an underwater cave in the Amazon.

The cave became narrow and we couldn't swim as quickly. Our arms needed to stay very close to our bodies to fit through. We instinctively used our hands like fins to push forward while our feet kicked. I slowly let out my breath little by little as my mother had taught me years before when we had dug for clams at the ocean. The trick is to release a bit of air every ten seconds. This taught me to focus more on my task and less on everything else that might distract me.

Finally we reached the surface. Sergio and I came up with a gasp, and Tavi barely breathed in. He must have done this many times before. The sun had just begun to rise and the bats had already been shrieking. We swam to the shallow end of the pond and climbed out. That's when I realized that it wasn't the same pond we had jumped into. This place looked different somehow. The flowers smelled different; the foliage was more colorful, unlike anything I had ever seen or read about. The trees looked larger, much older.

Tavi urged us on speaking in a language that I had never heard before. It didn't sound like Portuguese, French, Spanish, or English. His voice hummed as he spoke. It sounded almost like a song. I didn't think it was possible to speak and hum at the same time but it looked natural and easy for Tavi. I remembered my father waking me from the dream and I wondered if *I* had spoken *this* language. Could we be getting closer to Mom? I caught up to Sergio. I needed answers and he seemed to know what was going on.

"Well? Are you gonna tell me anything?"

"Can't you hear him?" Sergio asked.

"No. I can't. I can't hear anyone who hasn't spoken for hours."

"I guess I can hear him speak to me without having to actually talk," Sergio rambled. "It's some kind of telepathy. That's how I knew to keep quiet when Dad was captured. Bats are nocturnal. They have poor eyesight but could hear very well. And did you happen to know that they are the only flying mammals that…"

"Telepathy! Huge, nocturnal bats! Are you kidding me?"

"That's how I knew his name was Tavi and that we'd be jumping into the water to get to his village on the other side," Sergio said. "He's going to keep us safe."

"What will happen to Dad?"

"Shhhhh, I'm listening to Tavi," Sergio said, holding his hand in front of my face. "It's hard for me to hear."

Sergio began to fill me in as we walked through a patch of flowers. I had suddenly smelled the aroma of cotton candy. I stopped short. This was the sugary smell in my dreams! It was pungent but I couldn't tell exactly which flower it was coming from. I immediately went to the largest flower. Such a strong odor must come from a flower of this size. Strangely, it had no odor. I reached for a beautiful pink and orange flower, sniffed, and pulled away. The musky scent made me feel sick. It all seemed familiar and it reminded me of the story of The Three Bears. It was probably the smallest, simplest flower that had the sweetest smell but before I could find out, Tavi had pulled me away.

We reached a village. As we walked through, we were instantly surrounded by children. They hummed and spoke softly to one another as more and more emerged from the tree dwellings. Each one climbed down with expertise and used their fingers and toes to grip the vines. They reminded me of gorillas as they swung from the vine to another with ease. No one seemed clumsy or awkward. There were children of all ages but it seemed that none were more than fifteen years old. A young girl handed us a bowl with a delicious paste and we ate feverishly. We sat under a tree with plenty of shade, feeling ten degrees cooler and more comfortable than being out in the blazing heat. The children spoke for some time, and Sergio nodded occasionally to respond. It seemed that they could not read Sergio's mind as he could theirs. He had to play charades with the group to describe our father and mother's disappearance. They began to hum louder when we mentioned our missing parents, and when Sergio took out his family photo from his journal, the noise ceased instantly. They must have recognized our mother. Tavi looked at Sergio and my brother nodded. We were led to a tree house and our hands were placed on the vines. Just as my fingers enclosed the vine, I was yanked up into the tree dwelling by two strong children. Their strength was unlike any child I had ever seen. We were led to handmade beds stuffed with real feathers. I slept for hours and woke up sometime in the early evening. I made my way out of the tree house and found Sergio with a thin stripe tattooed across his forehead, beads around his wrists, and a crown of leaves and flowers.

"What are you, their king or something?"

"Actually, I think I am," he giggled. "Apparently, they've been waiting for me for years. For some reason, they say that I'm their guide, whatever that means. I wasn't telepathic at home but it began the minute we flew over Brazil. Yesterday, I knew what you wrote in your journal but I had to see for myself," Sergio said.

"Why didn't you tell me?"

"I don't know," he said, shuffling his feet. "You'd just make fun of me."

"You're probably right. Sorry." I felt myself blush.

Tavi led us to a clearing with a fire pit surrounded by fifty or sixty children. They stopped humming and a few led Sergio to a giant flat agate that resembled a green throne. More beautiful, glittering agates surrounded the pit, casting reflections on the children's faces. Sergio was elevated higher than the rest of the group and I shuddered to think of how elevated his ego would become.

I sat next to Sergio and watched the children dance to their own music. It sounded exotic, different from anything I had ever heard. Each instrument made a resonating sound like the howler monkeys but the tone was soothing. The musicians, some no more than six years old, played like experts, making it look so easy. I took lessons in the flute when I was nine and found it to be really difficult but the children were masterful at everything they had done.

The children experimented with my lip gloss. It was funny to watch them apply it to one another's lips and marvel over the shimmer and color.

As the sun began to set, the music grew quieter. The children began to speak less and the hum became softer. Finally, there was no sound at all. The children were settling down around the fire and they became still. "What's going on, Sergio?" I whispered. He put his finger to his lips and two other children placed their hand in the air, sideways and with the palm towards me as if they mimed their hand over my mouth. This was their way of keeping me from speaking. The children had begun to sign to one another as the light from the sky faded to dark.

Tavi stood up and had begun a routine of charades. He told a story and used his body to communicate. It was difficult to understand everything he was trying to say, but in time I began to pick up on his language. He danced around the fire and showed happiness and freedom. Then he crouched down low with his hands over his head and showed fear. He looked up towards the sky and hid his face in his hands. Suddenly his arms whipped from his sides and flapped as a bat would. He flailed about and raised his hands in the air and walked around the outer circle. He looked as if he were playing Duck-Duck-Goose as he carefully selected his victim. The children hovered over and hoped that they would be overlooked. Without warning, Tavi grabbed at the oldest child and yanked her from her seat. She covered her mouth with her hand so as not to scream. The children looked very serious. It did not look like they were playing a game. Tavi was trying to tell us what had happened to the people of his village.

"All of the parents were taken. The children could always run faster and could hide in small places but the parents weren't quick enough," Sergio said.

When the charade ended, the girl sat down. I noticed something she was wearing as the fire reflected light on the silver charm. I jumped up.

"That was my mother's bracelet! Where did you find that?" I squealed.

The children jumped to their feet and had begun to kick dirt on the fire to squelch the flames. They took off in different directions. I tried to reach for the girl but I was dragged towards a tree dwelling. When Tavi, Sergio, and I got inside, Sergio began to speak for Tavi. He was very quiet, very mature, and very unlike my brother.

"Listen Larissa, you have to be absolutely quiet when the sun sets or the village will be attacked. The bats may not see well but they'll find you if you make noise," Sergio said, whispering.

"Did you see that girl's bracelet? It was Mom's. You know, the one grandmother gave to her when Mom was a kid."

"Yeah, that's Tavi's sister, Mori. She's the medicine girl. Both of her parents were taken and now she cares for the children in the village," Sergio said. He looked over at Tavi and motioned to his wrist. He waited as Tavi responded to his question. Sergio smiled ear to ear and could hardly contain his excitement. He whispered, "Mori didn't *find* that bracelet. Mom was here!"

"Duh, they recognized Mom from the picture you carry. Guess that's why they made you their king," I said.

"Actually, they crowned me because of my doodles in my field journal. The called me *The Sun Guide*. They didn't say anything about Mom," Sergio said matter-of-factly.

Sergio continued to communicate with Tavi who had begun charades again. He held his arms out wide and glided across the room. He pulled his arms in tight and rolled across the floor. He stepped out of his cocoon, stood tall, and practically glowed as if to say someone extraordinary walked out. He pointed with his middle finger, something typically done by a Brazilian just as an American would point with his index finger. He motioned toward the clay bowls on a table made up of bamboo, banana leaves, and vines. Inside the bowls were mashed up roots and plants. But what really jumped out was a pestle made of ivory.

"That's Mom's pestle," I whispered excitedly. I started to pace and started biting my nails – another terrible habit. I was lost in my own thoughts. Mom's plane crashed. She was rescued by Tavi and Mori and brought back here, where she did some work with the plant life.

"That's right," Sergio said. "Tavi told me that they saw Mom's plane crash just north of here and they carried Mom from the wreckage." He stopped to listen to Tavi's silent voice and continued, "She was injured badly, but Mori nursed her back to health and that's why she couldn't contact anyone."

A loud shriek was heard above the trees. Tavi made the silent gesture again. Mom must have known not to scream. That was why everyone was silent in the dreams. It sounded like eight or ten bats above, circling and clawing at the rooftops. We waited in silence for what felt like an hour until the bats were gone. Sergio and I slept restlessly. I had another dream; they were coming in waves now.

Everything was white: walls, floor, tables, even clothing. There were no windows and no voices. Everything was silent except for a strange whirring sound. I was seeing through Mom's eyes again. She was frantically looking around, investigating every corner of the room and looking for a fault somewhere. She was trying to escape, but from what?

Chapter 6
The Trap

"Mom's still alive!"

"Yes," Sergio hissed, pulling his fist in with victory.

"She's in a white room without windows," I said remembering the details.

"That's weird," Sergio said. He was being adorned with tiny white flowers and blue beaded necklaces. "We're in the middle of the Amazon. What do you mean *white* room?"

I couldn't help but roll my eyes while four and five-year-old children began combing through his wavy hair. My brother, King of the Amazon Children! "I know but that's where she was. She was looking for a way to escape. She's in danger."

"You mean other than her plane crashing, being attacked by a gigantic bat and being kept against her will?" he said, sounding smug.

I nudged his arm. The children began nudging one another playfully with smiles that seemed to have been hidden for a long time. They had a beautiful olive skin, much like our mother, and bright, gleaming eyes full of love and kindness. Their voices were melodious and their body language was graceful. They moved as if they floated and ran at an amazing speed.

They developed strategies in the Amazon that kept them alive without their parents' help for months. When the bats hovered, I noticed how quickly the children dispersed. No child ran with another. There didn't seem to be a buddy system, and the littlest ones were just as quick and self-sufficient as the older children. They all assumed the roles of their parents and hunted for food, gathered fruits and vegetables, and carried on the lifestyles that their parents would have. They took their daily chores seriously and worked very hard throughout the day. They all seemed so... mature.

After my brother was adorned and looked completely ridiculous, we went outside again and gathered at the clearing where the children sat around Sergio in crouched positions. The humming began. My brother began a charade, planning the attack.

Four children dragged netting found in my mother's airplane, which held cargo in place during turbulence. Sergio inspected the netting. He referred to his survival guide to devise a trap. The children were given jobs and the work began.

Mori took me by my hand and led me off into the brush. Although she was very slender, she had a round face. She wore her hair back and tucked under, creating an exotic twist resembling the simple white flower I had seen earlier. She was tattooed as they all were but had a beautiful design of the sun on the back of her neck which seemed familiar. She had begun to dig up roots embedded in an old gnarled tree. She led me back to the dwelling and used my mother's pestle to grind the roots to a mashed pulp. The smell was also familiar. She added some paste that we ate the night before and sprinkled a dried herb over the top. She smeared the paste on banana leaves and motioned for my help. Together, we worked until we were called from a child in the distance. She quickly gathered the pasted leaves and placed them in a bowl. She motioned to the sun and danced her fingers from the sunlight to the bowl, expressing to me that the paste needed to dry.

We stood at the edge of the dwelling floor. She wrapped her arm around the vine and slid down effortlessly. I looked ridiculous as I wobbled onto the vine and awkwardly made my way down hand-over-hand. Suddenly I lost grip of the vine and plunged towards the ground. I shut my eyes tight and prayed for a soft landing and found myself caught safely in Mori's arms. The look of surprise on my face must have been pretty funny. Mori giggled and placed me carefully onto my feet, which were still rubbery from the fall. I nodded to thank her and she nodded back.

We walked back to the fire pit where the children were working. The net trap was set in the brush where the adults were captured. The older children were making slings. Two children taught Sergio and me the technique of sling shooting. A stone was enclosed in a soft leather hammock with vines attached. The idea was to swing the stone like a lasso over our heads quickly to build up speed. Once the target was in view, in this case animal skins stuffed with banana leaves, we snapped the sling forward which hurled the stone towards the target. Each child was an expert as they nailed the target, knocking it to and fro.

Sergio called a gathering by blowing into a wooden wind instrument which made a low-pitched tone. We gathered around the stone pit and ate dinner which consisted of the delicious paste, some sweet fruits, and fish caught by some of the girls. A huge animal was dragged in from the brush and thrown near the pit. I let out a scream. The children laughed and I felt myself blush.

"It's a capybara. It's the world's largest rodent. That one looks pretty big. Tavi caught this one while we were sleeping," Sergio said. The boys hung the rodent by its legs, dangling from a long, heavy piece of wood. They slid one side of the wood into a channel carved in a post while the other side was placed in the opposite side. The contraption hung over the fire pit.

"I'm not eating that."

"You don't eat it. The meat is too tough. They just use its fat for medicines," Sergio said.

"How long was Tavi gone for?"

"Almost all night. Tavi doesn't sleep every night like the villagers do. He said he sleeps for two hours every fourth or fifth sunset. It's all he needs. His father was the village owl and this was passed onto Tavi. He has his father's *poderes* of strength and energy, and Mori has her mother's *poderes*," Sergio said.

"Let me guess, the *poderes* of strength and healing."

"Yup. Mori's mother was still here when Mom arrived at the village. Tavi said that Mom was unconscious but when she awoke, Mori was the one who had set her broken arm and stitched her wounded leg. That's why she wears Mom's bracelet. I guess it was her way of thanking Mori," he said.

"Hmm. So much of this place seems familiar. Do you recognize this paste? I know I've had it somewhere."

"Yeah I noticed. But I don't remember seeing it before," he said.

The afternoon rolled on and the children trained by practicing their unique *poderes*. Tavi and Mori did an amazing acrobatic and balancing act. Mori would hold her brother's entire body up above her head while he balanced on one of her slender arms. She then began to move in a way that made me think of a ballet dancer holding a bird in her hand. Another boy and his younger brother were able to blow a dart through a long, hollow tube of bamboo across the length of a football field. They always hit their target, which was nothing more than a small flame from a candle made out of capybara fat. Another family of sisters tossed about objects to one another, sort of like a juggling routine. I'd seen this before in the circus and by street performers until I realized that it was random and unplanned. That was when the objects were hurled toward the other children at an amazing and frightening speed. The children, busy with their own feats, caught and returned every object before I was able to blink. Flying stones, small, fiery torches, and darts flew around and I huddled up with my brother so as not to interfere and possibly get impaled. Each child demonstrated some amazing talent and no two were alike.

"Tavi told me that they acquired their *poderes* from their parents, the same way you can wind up with your mother's eyes and your father's build. He said that their *poderes* were a curse and caused trouble with other villages. They were different, stronger, and faster, and it confused and frightened neighboring tribes. They were persecuted

68

and exiled so they traveled deep into the Amazon and were never seen again. He said that this is why the tribe has no name," Sergio said.

"So they just left? No questions asked? No fights?"

"They're peaceful people," he said. "Remember the older kid that lived down the street, Tyler Grant? He was different? He was left out and ignored because people didn't like that he was quiet one minute and yelling the next about simple things like his pencil point breaking? Yeah well, he's now fifteen and studying at Harvard. Now he's this genius mathematician." He ate the last of his fruit and paste and stopped short. "That's it. This tastes something like the protein shake Mom always made us for breakfast."

Sergio turned to Tavi and pointed to the mixture. He pointed to Mori and motioned for her to come over. She hadn't exchanged a word but continued to communicate with my brother with her thoughts. This waiting definitely required patience. Mori untied a pouch from her waist belt and pulled out a pinch of green and white herbs. She separated the herbs with her fingers and pointed toward each one. Sergio sniffed the herbs. He nodded and Mori nodded back, returning to her work.

"Mori described the ingredients and it winds up that many of them are in Mom's shake. The chemical combinations of two acidic ingredients, an herb made from a hybridized flower and..." Sergio continued.

"If you spoke in Portuguese, I'd probably understand you better."

"Sorry," he giggled. It was nice to see him smile again. "Okay, basically Mom used ingredients from the rainforest to make our breakfast shakes. Let's see... it was a mixture of mango juice, lemon juice, water, and a few Brazilian herbs. The only thing that's strange is that one ingredient is only found this deep in the Amazon, your cotton candy flower that you dreamed about. It isn't found anywhere else in the world because it was created by the hands of these villagers and their ancestors."

I remembered learning about this in Earth science class. We cross-pollinated one kind of flower with another, producing a new variety of flower called a hybrid. It didn't seem that complicated but my flowers didn't grow and my lab partner blamed me for not watering them before the vacation. But it didn't explain how Mom had the same dried flowers at home. She didn't know about the hidden village. No one knew these people even existed.

Mori pulled a dried white flower from her medicine pouch and showed it to me. It was the same, simple flower I had seen before. "Maybe someone left the village and brought this flower with them to trade."

"I doubt that. If you were in hiding and didn't want the outside world to find you, would you leave with a piece of evidence that would lead people to your doorstep?" He was right. They were very protective of their people. No one would have taken a chance and put their village in jeopardy. "Besides, Tavi said that the flower can only grow in the soil from this area of the rainforest. It's rich with minerals. When the villagers found this place, they could see the difference in the foliage. The nutrients in the soil could not be found anywhere else," he said.

After dinner, Sergio, Tavi, Mori, and I went into the brush. We set up the trap and hid the netting under leaves. The sun had just started to set.

"We need to get back to the dwellings," I said.

"Actually, we need to lure the bats," Sergio said.

"What? Are you kidding? I'm not letting you be the bait! I can't believe they actually would allow you, their *King*, to do this!"

"Well," he paused, "you're right; they wouldn't allow it, so I volunteered you for the job."

"What!" I was completely shocked. My brother, my ally, my blood, would volunteer his sister! "What happened to devotion and family sticking together? Oh no, I'm not doing this."

"Listen Larissa, nothing is going to happen to you. You just have to stand there; we will take care of the rest." He motioned toward the other children.

"That's reassuring," I said sarcastically. "Where will you be?"

"There," he said. He was pointing to a lean-to. I noticed that they were built throughout the village and wasn't sure why until that moment. Each time the bats arrived, the children split up and crawled under the lean-tos when there was no time to reach a dwelling. It was a simple design. Two sticks held up two corners of a flat roof made from thatched leaves and vines. A hole was dug into the ground and the children jumped into it when they were in danger. The sticks folded inward which dropped the roof over the hole like a small cellar door. I had seen something like this in Sergio's survival guide. They were camouflaged well and made the perfect hiding spot when necessary. I imagined the creepy insects inside the hole and shivered.

I could see the intensity in Tavi and Mori's eyes. I thought about my parents and wished I could help them. I thought about the white room and how I felt desperate to get out. I paced back and forth, wringing my hands until I had a moment of clarity. If I planned to help save my parents, then we'd have to start somewhere. "Fine, I'll do it. But you better be there to save me if they get too close."

"We will," he said. Sergio wrapped his arms around me, pinning my arms tight against my body.

"Okay, enough." I said irritably. Tavi and Mori stood behind me and placed their hands on my shoulders. Their simple gesture comforted me.

The sun had set and I was thankful for the moon's light. Suddenly, I felt completely alone. My teeth had begun to chatter. Sergio whispered for me to start making noises.

"Alright," I hissed. "Shush. Give me a minute."

I began to sing *Somewhere over the Rainbow* as loud as I could. Of course, I wasn't singing in my best voice but it wasn't that bad. It wasn't long before two gigantic bats hovered above the treetops. They silently stalked their prey. They were so quiet. and I wondered if they were there watching us plan all along. I shrieked. My instinct was to run for my life, but I remembered to hold my ground so the trap could work. One bat remained high up in the branches with its claws gorged into the trunk of the tree I stood beneath and watched while the other swooped down to attack. I ducked and rolled but the bat was relentless. It continued to swoop down toward me, again and again.

"It's not working, Sergio," I said panicking.

"Stop ducking," he hissed back from his safe and distant lean-to.

"Are you crazy or something?" I screeched.

Just then, the bat swept down and landed directly over the netting which had been camouflaged with leaves. Something came over me. I stood with my eyes closed, completely still. Suddenly I felt powerful, unafraid. I slowly opened my eyes to find the creature not five feet away, legs crouched and ready to pounce. I felt something close tightly over my ribcage and instantly I was pulled up into the tree. I screamed, imagining the bat snatching me up into the sky the same way my mother had been. But it was Mori. She had climbed the tree and lassoed me in an instant, yanking me off the ground before I was harmed. The net closed over the bat and trapped it. Tavi and Sergio raced out from the lean-to as the second bat took off. The other children in the village came running out to help. All that time I felt alone, when in truth, I was completely surrounded by the children. They had all been there to help carry out Sergio's plan. With Mori's strength, Tavi's skills, and of course my foresight, we captured one creature. Why? I had no idea, but we had done it nevertheless.

A teenage boy approached the captured bat slowly and carefully. He squatted low to the ground and inched toward the bat on its right side. The bat fixed its gaze on him. He slowly lifted his arms with palms out, this time with his fingers in opposite directions and wrists locked. His body swayed while he hummed. In time, the hostile bat quickly grew quiet and still. It lowered its head and revealed a collar with a small box buried within its coarse hair. The boy reached into the netting and released the collar carefully. He quickly pulled his hand away before the bat's fangs could clamp down on his hand. The bat was still in a trance long enough for the boy to get the box. The children released the netting to free the creature. A group of girls nudged its body with sticks, waking it from its dazed state. It opened its mouth wide and screeched at such a deafening pitch that we all covered our ears. It flapped its wings frantically and dug its claws into the loose soil. A few children were scraped and cut from the struggle but managed to break free from its grip. Finally, it was free from the netting and it took off into the night sky.

The children gathered up the netting and quietly went back to their dwellings where we all slept, except for Tavi. It was a long night but it wasn't Tavi's night to sleep. He spent the next few hours inspecting the box. I watched him until my eyes closed. I was hoping to avoid nightmares but welcomed dreams of my parents. "Please," I prayed, "let them be alright."

When I woke, I gathered my thoughts and woke Sergio who had been sleeping soundly.

"Get up." I nudged him. "Ask Tavi if Mom put herself in danger on purpose."

Sergio spoke to Tavi telepathically. Tavi spoke, this time in English. His accent was heavy but he spoke rather well for someone who just picked up the language. "When your mother healed, she learned how our people disappeared. She welcomed the bats to take her as well. She was silent. She knew we would have tried to stop her."

We were stunned. "How long have you been able to speak English?"

"Your mother taught me," Tavi said.

"So, you learned the English language in a week?" I was skeptical.

"A few days, really," he said. He laughed because of my astonished look on my face.

"I have to do exactly what Mom did. I have to be captured. It's the only way I can help our parents."

"Hold on. If you get captured, you may never get back," Sergio said solemnly.

"It's the only chance we've got. I've seen Mom in my dreams. I could find her."

"Then I'm going with you," he said. "You'll need my help."

Just then, Tavi reached for the box he had inspected for the last few hours. The lock had been pried open, exposing a red and green light. The green one was lit and was blinking. "It says here, 186 megahertz. I guess that means it works on radio waves. I read all about this. The green light is blinking, which means it's activated. And it also means that someone on the other end is in control of the bats. Once we removed the collar, it was freed, so someone is going to be pretty angry that they've lost one of their vampire slaves," Sergio said.

"Good. Then they'll send more."

"We need a new plan. You can't go alone and unarmed. We have to talk to the others." Tavi nodded and left to gather the children for another meeting.

"Are you sure about this?" Sergio asked.

"Never more positive," I assured him.

We gathered for our final plan and Sergio discussed the details with the children. A low hum came from his throat and he spoke to the children using their own language. It was in bits and pieces but I was mostly impressed that he had developed this ability in such a short time. He had two voices overlapping, humming and speaking simultaneously. He turned to me and found me staring completely and pleasantly surprised.

"Interesting," was all I could utter. My brother chuckled and headed toward the stream which ran throughout the village. He filled a canteen with water and sipped it slowly.

The villagers worked for hours. Mori and I checked the children who had injuries from the bat attack. She used the pasted banana leaves that we made together on their scrapes to help heal and prevent infections. That evening, we checked the wounds which were completely healed, leaving behind tiny pink scars.

"Wow! That stuff really works!"

Mori nodded and whispered, "Yes, it does."

She had spoken English as well. "How did you know…"

"Your mother is a good teacher," she said. "We learned to be careful. The jungle has ears. We will never be safe from the world of man. This is why we speak our own language."

I must have looked confused. She continued working and I began piecing it all together. The attacks must have gone on for quite some time before, possibly for decades. They have their own language to keep their lives as secretive as possible. They knew they were being watched. But who was watching them? And why?

In the late afternoon, the children gathered for the last time in front of the fire for something called a wishing ceremony. It was what the villagers did for centuries before a hunt. The girls stood up and gathered in a circle around the fire with their left hand resting on the right shoulder of the girl in front. As they stepped in silence, they would turn their bodies to face outward and would turn back in, again and again crouching lower as they finished a full circle. It was not a graceful dance but it was swift and fluid. When they were in a crouching position, they slowly began to rise up until they made their final rotation. Mori described this as a circle never to be broken.

Next, the boys stood in a circle, spread out wide so that they could not touch. Two boys on opposite sides jumped over the fire, switching places while the others made a spear-throwing motion with a stick. The stick had leaves attached to one side and they waved it through the air in perfect unison. The boys tossed the sticks into the fire and opened their arms wide with faces towards the sky. They swayed to and fro in rhythmical patterns.

The boys gathered dirt from their feet and one by one they threw the dirt onto the fire, squelching the flames until we sat silently in complete blackness.

Chapter 7

The Glass Room

We began preparing, everyone busy with his or her task. I stared into the jungle and hoped it wouldn't be my last time looking at its beauty. I silently acknowledged the world around me. It was a place I could never imagine, a home to plant and animal species that had never been discovered. But as awesome as it was to witness a place so novel, I couldn't appreciate any of it without my parents by my side. They were in danger and I was afraid I would never see their faces again. I would feel better if I had dreamed last night but I couldn't sleep.

"I let them down. I couldn't sleep, so I couldn't dream."

"It's okay. Dreaming is more an art than a science. Your subconscious mind creates a story and we can never predict when, where, or what you will dream of," Sergio said.

"Ah, so wise, sensei." I bowed at the waist as I had seen in old Kung Fu movies. A young girl handed me some items and gestured how each one is used. A fine red powder would turn into fire… somehow. It was poured into a leather pouch and was tied to my waist. "Great, I'm a ticking time bomb."

"It will only ignite if you wrap it in a leaf from a graviola tree," Sergio explained.

"Oh, I feel much better," I said sarcastically.

Sergio was given the leaves to hold as it would probably have been dangerous for me to carry. He was also given a very long lianas vine for climbing. Tavi carried dried fish, a long spear made from bamboo, a sharpened stone, and a belt of tiny spears made from whittled wood which had been tied around his waist. Mori carried her sling and a green herb, much like the herbs in my mother's kitchen cabinet.

The children waited until evening to offer one another luck. It was a tradition to do this at sunset and would have been considered bad luck to do this any time before. A girl about Sergio's age had given me my own tattoo on my hand. She used a slimy black ink made from water and crushed roots. The needle was from a bird talon that was tiny and hollow. She poked the nail into my skin and I was barely able to feel the sting. When she finished, I looked down to find a beautifully intricate cotton candy flower created by what looked like a single black line.

"It is your destiny," Mori said.

I thanked the young girl with a hug. She must have been surprised because she opened her eyes wide, smiled, and looked away bashfully.

We went to our designated spots to wait. Four rings made from pebbles were made on the ground, each circle overlapping another, symbolizing unity and strength.

"We are as one," Tavi said in plain English.

Mori called out in a pitch so high that it made my teeth hurt and within minutes, three bats nose-dived, wings pulled in and claws spread. I shut my eyes tight and threw my arms overhead as if that would somehow stop the creature from impaling me. The bat swept me off the ground with such force that it squeezed the air from my lungs. I gasped over and over again until I was able to finally breathe. My muscles locked as I watched the forest floor appear further and further away. I flew past the trees, which was just a dark blur. My heart pounded and I was afraid I would pass out but I forced myself to stay alert. I looked to my right to see Sergio being carried by a second bat. He was doubled over while gigantic claws wrapped around his waist as if he were a branch from a tree. Sergio lifted his head, spotted me, and waved. It was just his way of saying he wasn't hurt, but I wasn't amused.

The third bat held Tavi and Mori. Tavi and Mori were gripped over their shoulders and under their arms the same way you'd be harnessed on a rollercoaster. They were expressionless.

The bats passed over what appeared to be a canyon and nose-dived directly down into a river at the bottom. We were sure to be splattered at this speed but just as we were to hit the river, the bat placed its wing over my head as a shield. I screamed louder than I ever had before. I broke the record of all screams and even my own ears were pounding. I hadn't had enough time to hold my breath when we hit the water but it was no matter. We came up so quickly inside a cave that I had barely gotten wet. Before I knew it, I was dropped on a precipice. The cave was monstrous and, for a moment, I felt like I was on another planet. The stalagmites shot up from the cave bottom, some standing as high as a tree. The stalactites hung from the roof as sharp as icicles. The orange and brown colors swirled throughout the cave walls. It was cold and damp. Seconds later, my brother was dropped beside me with a thud and Tavi and Mori followed. We all were stunned and stared in silence and disbelief; everyone that is, except my brother who was already sweeping himself off and analyzing the situation.

"Whoever sent the bats will be coming for us, so let's get a move-on," Sergio said.

The creatures disappeared into a small cavern and Tavi began making a lasso with a vine. Mori took the vine and, with all of her strength, she threw it upward until it snagged in the fissure of a boulder. She climbed first. She was the strongest and also the lightest weight. If it didn't hold her, it wouldn't hold any of us. She climbed until she reached the top, tugged the vine twice, indicating that it was safe, and my brother began to climb. Sergio wasn't a good climber and lacked the strength of a ten-year-old. He did everything he could to get out of gym class. I always told him that he needed more exercise but he just rolled his eyes and kept reading his books. Tavi began to climb, passing over Sergio, using the rocks for leverage and allowed my brother to climb on his back for the rest of the journey up the vine. Now it was my turn.

I grew closer to the top when suddenly I was torn from the rope. I was ripped so hard that my hands were burned. The bat shrieked as we flew a few feet above the stalagmites. I pulled my knees in and shut my eyes until I was released. I fell two or three feet onto a steel plate the size of my bedroom. As I tried to stand up, the floor lifted off the ground and I noticed its chains. "An elevator? In a cave?" I rose higher and higher until it stopped with a jolt. I squatted quickly so I wouldn't fall. Large steel doors slid open like a scene from one of Dad's old science-fiction movies. A bright light glared and I couldn't see who or what was inside. Hands reached out and grabbed me. I was relieved that they were human hands and not claws, or worse!

I was brought through another door and into a bright room which my eyes needed to adjust to. I blinked a few times until I was able to see clearly. The room was completely white except for a black cabinet in the far corner. There was a huge water tank in another corner and a cage in another. I was shoved into a chair in front of a long table and my wrists and ankles were forced into straps pulled so tightly that I couldn't budge. I stared at a curtained window. I expected the curtains to open and I was petrified to see what might have been on the other side but it remained closed. A voice came over a speaker. "Hello, dear," the voice said. It was difficult to know if it was a man or woman, but thank goodness it was human. "Just relax and be patient. We have a few questions," the voice continued.

"Where am I?" I asked.

"What color are you thinking of?" the voice asked, ignoring my question.

"What? What do you mean? Where are my parents?" I tried to stand but the straps held me in place.

"What color, Larissa?" asked the voice calmly.

"How do you know my name? Are you people insane! Let me go!" I tried to wriggle but hands came down hard on my shoulders.

"Answer the question, dear," the voice said. "What color?"

"I don't know… magenta?" I was being sarcastic, of course.

"Very good," the voice said. "What shape are you thinking of, Larissa?"

"Who are you?" I asked.

"Answer the question," the voice commanded.

"An amoeba, okay?" Now I was enraged. "Where is my mother? You can't keep us here!"

"You're doing fine, Larissa. Just one more question. What number are you thinking of from one to a thousand?"

"Are you listening to me? Let me out of here!" I screamed.

"Answer the question," the voice said, losing patience. I feared that matters were going to get worse if I didn't cooperate.

"Four and a half, okay? Now, where am I?"

"Excellent, dear. You may take her to her chambers," the voice said.

The cuffs were removed and I was whisked out of my chair so fast that I never had a chance to say another word. I was taken down a long hallway and pushed into a familiar room with padded white walls. It was the same room from my dreams. My eyes closed as I sunk to the ground. I had no sense of time and didn't know if I was waiting for minutes or hours. A small door low on the ground slid open and a tray with a turkey sandwich, milk, and baby carrots was pushed through. The tiny steel hatch slid closed without a word from the delivery person. I gobbled down the food within a minute. I had no idea when I last ate and decided to take the risk of it being poisoned.

I hoped that Sergio, Tavi, and Mori were all right. I contemplated my escape, but the room had no windows or a door handle, and I knew it was completely out of my hands. A prisoner could never know the time of day because there was no clock. It seemed completely soundproof, so I probably could scream my head off and no one would know it. I couldn't tell the time based on the meal because it was the same meal each time, which I was growing tired of by the third round.

Finally, I slept. It was a deep sleep, probably lasting for hours. I dreamed of my father. He was whispering something. For the first time in my life, I couldn't hear his voice. Was I losing my *poderes*? I tried to read his lips but just couldn't understand him. I felt helpless. Another dream began. It was my mother. She was making something with a mortar and pestle. She was grinding a white powder. She looked up from her concoction and looked as if she was staring directly into my eyes. She looked at me and shifted her glance away and then back to me again. Then she continued to work. It was strange but I knew she was trying to tell me something.

I woke up to the small hatch sliding open again. I jumped at my chance to escape. My feet were pressed against the door, and as soon as I saw a hand push the tray of food through the miniature steel hatch, I pulled his fingers with one hand and his wrist with the other. I surprised myself as I yanked his arm in as far as I could and bent it upward towards the ceiling, leaning all of my weight against it. I could barely hear the guard cry out through the heavy steel. I put my ear very close to the opening and said, "Let me out of here."

I heard faint shuffling behind the door and knew there was something else happening out there. It was Mori wrestling the guard down while Sergio was fiddling with the lock. "Quickly."

"I'm going as fast as I can. It's a combination lock, like a safe," Sergio said. "Put your ear to the door and listen."

"What should I be listening for?"

"You'll hear a louder click. As soon as you hear it, say stop," he said.

I placed my ear to the door and listened. I could hear faint ticking. Seconds passed until I heard a click. "Stop." I waited for an even longer time. "Stop." After the last click, I could feel the door unhinge and a gust of cool air entered my chamber.

"I found Mom! Let's go. She's locked up in a glass room," Sergio said.

My heart skipped a beat. I stepped over the guard who was completely unconscious. Mori dragged him into the white chamber, tucking his legs in so that we could lock him inside. We ran down the corridor toward a dead end. Tavi pointed to a steel air duct high on the wall. I was scared to death. "I'm not going to fit." Tavi boosted me up. Surprisingly, I slid inside easily. But it was only slightly wider than my shoulders, giving me a sick feeling. One by one, we slid inside the duct while Tavi, who was last, jumped up to the duct and dove inside with ease. Sergio led us through the narrow opening until we reached the next empty room.

"This should lead us through the whole compound. We'll find her but we can't let her know we're here or she may freak out," Sergio whispered.

We slithered through the duct for quite a while and finally passed over a stark white room enclosed with glass. I could see my mother through the vent. She looked worn out. Her hair was pulled back loosely, her skin appeared to be grey, and she looked thin. Her assistant, a native Amazonian woman, looked tattered as well. They were mixing chemicals and herbs. Mori and Tavi exchanged glances. "That is our mother," Tavi whispered.

I must have looked completely confused until I realized that they were referring to Mom's assistant. I hadn't really thought much about the parents of the village. I was so wound up with my own problems that I hadn't considered that the entire village had been torn apart when their parents were taken from them. The children all seemed so well adjusted and confident while I was an emotional wreck. In fact, the more I looked at Sergio, the more he seemed like them. Now he was sort of expressionless and stoic.

Sergio kicked my arm to move onto the next room. I stopped breathing and couldn't take my eyes off her. I wanted so badly to scream out to her but knew that would be a costly mistake. My mother rubbed her neck, stretched her arms, and rolled her head back. She suddenly opened her eyes and fixed her gaze directly toward the grate in which I was hidden. She seemed to know that we were up inside the duct. She looked at me just as she had done in my dream. I froze.

"She can't see you," Sergio whispered.

"She knows we're here."

While they tried urging me on, I stiffened my body for one last look. She darted her eyes over to a table where a single white flower lay. It was the cotton candy flower. She was trying to tell me something but I just couldn't understand what it all meant. Finally, Mori whistled and motioned for me to head toward the next opening. Mom had gone back to her work, so I reluctantly moved on. One by one Mori pulled us out and softened our landing with her strong arms. We ran down a hallway towards another hallway and stopped in the shadows before rounding the corner. A stocky guard was talking to another in higher command. They saluted and the man in charge spoke briefly and quietly. I listened carefully.

"Troy was last seen delivering the food to the prisoners. He must have gone back to the lab. You're on duty. Stay alert," said the guard in command.

"Yes sir," said the guard while the other saluted and walked through the doors.

I relayed the conversation to the others when the stocky guard walked off. He sauntered down the hallway, whistling as he passed from door to door. We had no idea which room our father was in and had to wait it out until mealtime, just as they had done when I was locked up. We sat in the shadows for at least an hour and prayed that we hadn't missed our window of opportunity. Our own bellies rumbled, telling us that we needed to eat. Tavi unwrapped the dried fish from a suede skin and Mori shared water from a leather pouch. I was still satisfied from my last turkey sandwich but they ate vigorously. After some time, a cart of food was wheeled in and the guard nodded at the attendant. He slipped his hand under the cellophane, swiped a carrot, and then began to deliver the meals one by one. We waited patiently for a familiar voice. Suddenly, after the sixteenth door, I heard my father's faint voice. He whispered but so low that I could hardly hear. An image of my father appeared as a mirage. He had moved his lips as he had done in my dream and his whispers made complete sense.

"Take the white flower. Hide it," my father said. "Take it."

My father knew I was here. He was relaying a message from Mom. I understood now what I needed to do. It was the cotton candy flower that was so important. I needed to get to it before someone else did.

"Let's go." I pulled Sergio by the arm and we all ran back to the duct. I explained along the way what I had seen and heard.

"Dad's alright!" he said.

"For now," I said. We returned to the vent that overlooked the glass room. My mother's body language told me she knew we were back. She tensed up and called out, "We're finished here."

A guard opened up the door on the far end of the room. Tavi and Mori's mother lifted a tray with a formula they had been working on. She put it down quickly as the Indian woman began to collapse. Mom held her up and said, "She's exhausted. We need your help." The guard closed the door behind him, lifted the tray, and commanded the two women to follow his lead. As my mother left the room, she whispered, "Larissa Listen," and proceeded to close the door behind her.

Sergio looked at me puzzled. "What did she…?"

"Shhh." I listened as a code was pressed into a keypad. Six numbers were pressed, making tones so low that it was undetected by the others. I hummed the tones so that we all could remember the sequence in case I had forgotten. When our mothers and the guard were gone, we crawled through the next vent opening and dropped down directly in front of the door to the glass room. I pressed all the numbers to hear each tone, and together we figured out the combination. The door unhinged and swung open. I ran in, grabbed the white flower, and ran out, tucking it deep inside my pocket.

We crawled back through the duct, back to where the chambers held our families. Mori took out her sling and, with precision, knocked the guard unconscious. Tavi grabbed the man's arms and dragged him into the shadows. They slid their arms into each chamber through the food hatch, grasping hands with the people from their village. Sergio and I ran to our father's chamber door and did the same. "She's alive, Dad. We found her!"

"Thank God," he breathed and bowed his head.

Chapter 8

The White Flower

I reached up to the combination lock on my father's cell and listened for the ticks and clicks. Just as I was getting to the last number, I heard footsteps. "Someone's coming. Hide!" We hid in the shadows again, awaiting another guard. Sergio and Tavi glanced at each other and both nodded in agreement.

"What?"

"Shhh," Sergio hissed.

We waited again. Two female guards appeared in the doorway. I heard them coming and silently alerted the others. The women were discussing politics and realized that there was no one on duty. One guard looked bewildered, the other one irritated.

"Where's Brand? He was supposed to take the graveyard shift," the bewildered guard said. She had a pretty face, not at all what I expected a villain to have.

"I am not covering for him again," the irritated guard said. Her expression was very telling about her personality. She had hard features, small eyes, and her hair was pulled back so tight that her face looked harsh.

They continued to walk through the dimly lit hallway while the irritated guard questioned the other of the whereabouts of the guard on duty. Suddenly she tripped over the feet of the unconscious guard. I had to muffle my laugh.

We all smiled for an instant but knew it was time to act quickly. Tavi slid a tiny spear from his belt. Each spear had been dipped into a brown liquid. He slid one into a hollow bamboo and *floop*! It shot out like a canon, hitting the irritated guard first. She looked dazed, rolled her eyes, and slumped over the chair behind her.

"Call for back-up," whispered the pretty guard, unaware that her partner had been hit. When she realized, she reached for her walkie-talkie. *Floop!* She too was out.

I breathed out as if I had been holding my breath for a while. We sat the guards up back to back, and Mori tied them up with a vine. She pulled tightly and attached the loose end to a thick metallic pipe that ran from ceiling to floor. "That'll hold them," Sergio said.

Tavi spoke to Sergio and I found that I was beginning to understand bits and pieces of their language.

"Did he just say that we're going to leave Dad and the others here?"

"We have to. We'll never be able to sneak them all out with guards crawling all over the place. We have to get Mom. She'll know what to do," Sergio said.

I was hesitant but I moved on. "What happened to the old saying, 'There's strength in numbers'?"

"No," he said. "We're noisier. The villagers move quietly in the rainforest. They are out of their environment now. They're confused and frightened."

He was probably right. Even Mori and Tavi seemed uncomfortable and looked out of place. We walked quickly through the dark passageways and came across a showcase of artifacts. It reminded me of a museum back home in Northfork that had a collection of Amazonian pottery, jewelry, and bits of tattered clothing. In fact it was too similar. Sergio and I stopped short and stared at the collection. Each village we had seen had their own distinct art. Their colors and patterns in their clothing were a characteristic of their tribe.

"These were stolen from our village," Mori said in English. Their village used muted colors and simple designs so as not to draw attention to themselves. There were delicate drawings that were created with a single line as the children had for their tattoos. The jewelry was crafted with beads made from fired clay and colored with muted reds and blues and strung together with shredded husks just like Tavi and Mori wore. I recognized the pottery and the leather pouches adorned in feathers and beads from the village. I turned to my brother who was smiling from ear to ear.

"My doodles!" he said. "Those are the exact drawings that I'd drawn in my journal." A tattered piece of leather was pinned to the showcase wall which displayed an elaborate design of the sun. It was an exact replica of Sergio's drawings. "I told you they've been waiting for me."

"How long ago were these stolen?" I asked.

"They were made long ago by my ancestors but were taken from our village before we were born," Tavi said.

"That's even before I was born! Incredible!" Sergio said.

"Our parents told us stories about people from other lands taking our possessions. A few items at first, but they warned us that it would not stop there. Soon the people would be greedy and would want more," Tavi said.

"Our people traveled deeper into the jungle and built the village again. This time, our dwellings are in trees. Our parents taught us how to defend ourselves, how to cook, make weapons, and hunt if we were ever in trouble. Many full moons passed and our parents began to disappear one by one," Mori said. We began to walk briskly through the corridors.

"How did my brother's drawings end up in there?"

"My ancestors have spoken about your brother for a long time. They said a boy who draws this sun will be our savior. Your photograph and your journal had the same drawings as my people have drawn for centuries. That was how we knew it was you who would lead us to freedom," Tavi said.

We reached another air duct. Tavi boosted us up and we crawled through quietly. A burst of air traveled through the vents, cooling our bodies off. My fear of closed-in spaces finally mellowed. We hovered over a room that had a strong smell of musk. Mori dropped down first to survey the room. She nodded, and one by one we dropped to the nearest tabletop. Across the room were cages filled with exotic animals. I recognized a few, like the toucan from my dreams and a tank of piranha, but there were some I had never seen before. Even Sergio was fascinated by the creatures.

"I never saw this species before," Sergio said. He was pointing to a white lizard with scaled wings. He walked past the cage to another and he gulped. It was a large grey monkey with a small beak. "It's a marsupial." He was pointing to its pouch which held three infants. I felt sorry for the caged animals and fed them a few pellets each. "We have to keep moving."

We slipped through the corridor and could hear a voice beyond a set of doors. We pushed open the doors a little at a time until we were safely inside. We were in the back of a massive lecture hall, much like the one my parents spoke at in the university. When Sergio and I were very young, our mother would take us to some of Dad's science lectures. He seemed very respected and my brother and I admired him. My mother was so proud that she beamed and nodded occasionally. We were too young to understand his lectures but Sergio took notes anyway.

Up in front was a woman in a white lab coat, speaking to a crowd of fifteen or twenty more people in identical white coats. Guards were scattered around the room in pairs. One seemingly important guard stood in the front, legs spread apart and arms crossed. We squatted quickly and crawled between two empty rows, waiting for something to happen.

The woman up front spoke with a British accent. "The flower is essential because of its ability to promote physical and mental growth. It's displayed differently based on the individual. The results are completely enigmatic."

"Who was she talking about? What individuals?"

"Why have the adults lost the ability to use their strengths?" a man in the back asked.

"It seems that their abilities dissipate as they grow older. It is my guess, based on Larissa's abilities, that the children have their strengths from a very early age and it peaks at pre-adolescence. According to the study on the young adults, it begins to fade sometime in their twenties. By the time they reach forty, the strength is gone," the speaker said. "My hypothesis proved to be incorrect. We've been studying the adults for a decade when we should have been studying the children."

"Why do we need Dr. Ricci?" a man asked with an Australian accent. "She's been working round the clock and the white flower has been making her very ill. She apparently doesn't know the formula. The flower has proven to be poisonous and has made the guards sick as well."

"Dione Ricci is the only one who we can communicate with. We cannot understand the natives' language but she does understand. She's had knowledge of the flower's potency for many years. She's been bringing it back to the United States," the speaker said.

"I truly doubt she'd make herself that ill just to protect the secrets of the flower," a woman said with a Russian accent. "She almost died twice."

The speaker scoffed, "I wouldn't count on it. She cares for these people and will protect them…"

An elderly woman interrupted, "We have been observing the Indian women making this paste for a decade. They all eat it, even the babies. The white flower has been used each and every time using the same combination of ingredients. What are we missing?"

"That is precisely why we hired you, Doctor Murphey. We are all scientists here for one purpose and one purpose only: to find the key to the tribes' superhuman abilities. But we are running out of time. If we fail to find the formula in the next few days, the experiments will be over." She looked down at her feet, took a deep breath, and looked up again. "We've been observing and collecting data on these people for thirty-two long years and I'm leaving no stone unturned. If Dr. Reinhardt can no longer fund this project, we all will be out of work," the speaker said.

A large guard entered through the front doors. He was wearing gold pins on the shoulders of his black uniform. "Dr. Ricci's daughter is under surveillance now." He pointed to two guards in the front corner of the room. "Get the girl."

The guards saluted and quickly left the room. The speaker continued to address the other doctors. "The Indians are useless to us. Therefore, the American woman and child will continue to be tested. They obviously have a deeper connection. Larissa read her mother's mind flawlessly. She is very powerful. I'd like to run a scan on her brain before we go in."

"What?" I jumped. "Go in? Go in where?"

Sergio put his hand over my mouth and said, "Did you see Mom when they were testing you?"

I shook my head no. She must have been the one on the other side of the window. I was reading her mind! Did she know I was there? Of course, they said my name like five times and she must have recognized my voice. Memories swam in and out of my head until I felt dizzy.

The lecture ended and the doctors filed out of the room. When the lights went down, we crept out to follow the crowd at a safe distance. I knew there would be chaos as soon as they realize I escaped from my chamber, so we had to act fast. The guards stopped in the hallway and blocked our path to the room that the speaker had entered from. We stayed back behind the corner wall and waited for our moment.

"Why did Mom and Dad want you to take the flower? Isn't it poisonous? Have we been poisoned all these years?" I started to panic.

"Uh, yeah," said Sergio. He put his hands around his throat, gasped for breath, and wheezed, "I'm dyin'. I'm dyin'."

"Your mother is a strong woman. She hasn't given up the formula because she is protecting our people. She's even willing to risk her life by misusing the flower," Tavi said.

"How can you misuse a flower?" Sergio said.

"Our ancestors created this unique flower. It keeps us healthy and strong. You must pick the flower in the evening, minutes before the petals close. It is the exact timing that is important. If the petals close, the pistil releases a clear liquid that protects it from nocturnal predators. It is poisonous and can make many animals very ill. In the daytime, the flower produces a beautiful, sweet smell, but if eaten, it can also make you ill. At sunset, when the smell dissipates and the pistil has not yet released its liquid, it is safe to pick. These scientists do not know this, and your mother has kept this a secret," Mori said.

The guards dispersed while two men in white coats rolled in a gurney with my mother strapped on. She appeared unconscious. They forced open the swinging doors into a laboratory. The doors remained open for a second or two, just enough time to see two tables with white sheets, four IV bags, lots of machines with blinking lights, and a nurse standing over a small cart with a syringe in her hand. "We must act quickly," Tavi said, already with his darts in hand. Mori had the sling and she handed me the green herb that she had tucked away in her belt.

"It will awaken your mother," she said.

Sergio counted, "One, two, threeeeee." We all ran towards the doors, ready for a fight.

Chapter 9

Our Escape

They were taken by complete surprise. Utter chaos broke out as we ran around the room hooting and hollering. Tavi drugged the two doctors and the nurse with his spear darts. Each one let out a tiny gasp while the brown, gooey drug immediately took effect. They dropped to the ground in what seemed like slow motion. Sergio and I quickly emptied the green herb onto the rolling cart which had numerous scalpels of all shapes and sizes, a long scissors, and a pile of gauze. "It looks like oregano. What are supposed to do with this?" I asked.

"I dunno. She probably has to ingest it," Sergio said.

I stuck my finger in the pile of the green, shredded, and dried mixture and rubbed it between my forefinger and thumb. It had a potent smell, much like lavender. I put it to my nose and inhaled deeply. My heart beat faster and the exhaustion I had felt faded instantly.

"I got it!" I took a pinch of the herb and held it up to Mom's nose and whispered into her ear, "Breathe deeply, Mom." She breathed in the aroma and instantly awoke from her drugged state. She needed us to help her sit up but Mori helped her off the gurney and onto her feet. She was confused and out of sorts but recognized us and extended her arms for a hug. Tears streamed down our faces and she whispered softly, "My babies."

Some say that we remember particular moments in life because our emotions were deeply touched. Extremely sad moments or deliriously happy moments are the most prominent. This was a moment that I will never forget for as long as I live. "Let's go find your father," she said.

We ran down the hallway, backtracking to the ventilation shafts. "I'll never fit in there," Mom said. Tavi and Sergio slid inside and closed the vent cover. "Find your father and meet us in the cave. I'm not finished here," Mom said.

Mori, Mom, and I ran to the lab and she punched in the code that she too remembered by its tone. The door opened and the animals became alert. We sensed their nervousness. She opened each cage to remove the homing device from the animals but did not release them. She quietly closed each cage.

"Why aren't you freeing them, Mom?"

"We're underground," she whispered. "What good is it to free them here? They can't be controlled without the collar. That's good enough for now. They'll be released later."

Just as we were about to head out, a group of guards appeared. "Stop right there, Dr. Ricci," a guard said.

"Don't move," the other said.

We were yanked out of the lab and brought to the glass room where Mom had spent weeks experimenting on the flower. The speaker was there, ordering the other doctors around. Mom, Mori, and I were dragged to the lab tables.

"We have very little time here, Dr. Ricci," the speaker said. "I have run out of patience. Your husband, the villagers, all of you will be set free if you finish the experiment. We know you have the answer. I suggest you work quickly."

Mom nodded and ground together some dried herbs. She squeezed the juices from two citric fruits and looked directly at me. She looked exhausted and very sad. She was completely powerless as she held out her frail hand to me.

"Give me the flower, honey," she said.

"No, Mom, we can't."

"It's okay. Give it to me," she said quietly.

I looked at Mori and back at my mother, then back at Mori, searching for an answer in their eyes. We can't really be giving up the secrets that kept this village alive for all of these generations. No tribe could have survived without resources from the outside world. They've lived and prospered in a place that was too dangerous and remote for anyone to live. They survived the dangers of intruders, wild animals, and sickness, and they managed to thrive without help from any other tribe. The white flower is the only thing that kept the villagers alive and now I'm handing it over to the bad guys?

"Trust me, Larissa. It will all be fine. Give me the flower," Mom said.

Suddenly I realized that my mother was speaking to me without moving her lips. I was reading her thoughts the same way Sergio had done! I tried not to smile and handed her the flower from my pants' pocket. It was shriveled and sticky but not poisonous. This flower must have been picked at the right time. She put the flower into the mixture and blended the ingredients with a little water.

The doctors held masks over their mouths, waiting for a poisonous gas to be expelled. When nothing happened, the speaker approached cautiously and sniffed the mixture and held it up to the light.

"I guess you've been holding out on us, doctor," she said. "Drink." She handed the glass to my mother. My mother put the glass to her lips and swallowed.

"Again," the speaker said.

She took a large gulp this time. "It's fine, Dr. Lake. I make this every morning for my family," Mom said.

Dr. Lake took the glass from my mother's hands and took a large sip. Then she finished the drink completely. A man stood at her side with a small recorder. "I feel energized. My heart is beating faster, not too much, but I feel alive, powerful. I feel like I could do anything." The other scientists were writing notes in their journals and one was tapping away at the keyboard which was hooked up to a monstrous computer. The speaker continued to describe the taste and texture. I could hear my mother. It was as if she had entered my mind.

"Only you can speak to Dr. Lake, Larissa. Project your thoughts onto her and she will think the poderes are hers," Mom said, staring directly into my eyes without speaking. *"Tell her that she is now telepathic and reading minds is just the beginning. Tell her that her poderes will develop over time and to be patient."*

I did exactly that. I took the doctor's hand and spoke to her with my thoughts. Dr. Lake's arm went up to hush the crowd. "I'm getting something. She's speaking to me," she said. She listened and shrieked, "It works! The flower works." She made fists in the air and shook them and then regained her composure. "Tell me, Dr. Ricci. *How* does it work?"

Mom explained the time frame in which the flower was poisonous and when it was safe. The doctors all nodded, eagerly taking notes and speaking at once. I heard Mom's voice in my head again. She said, *"Walk slowly towards the door."* I was the only one who stepped backward. She hummed a message to Mori who took the bag of brown powder from my belt, opened it, and cupped a handful, tossing it into the center of the room. The doctors froze. Mom grabbed a test tube with liquid and we backed our way towards the door. "Don't move," she said. I unlocked the door with the keypad and just as we had entered the hallway, Mom took a large gulp of water and sprayed it directly at the pile of brown powder. A large fire ignited and Mori pulled the door shut.

"But Mom, what about the fire? I asked. "Don't worry. The sprinklers will go on. No one will be hurt but it'll hold them for at least a minute or two," Mom said. We ran through the corridors. Mom leaned on Mori and me for support. We reached the chambers where my father was held. The male guard had just woken from his unconscious state and held the wound on his head. He looked completely puzzled as jets of water gushed from the overhead sprinklers. All of the chamber doors were open and empty. "Good job, Sergio," Mom said aloud, even though he was nowhere in sight. "Let's go." We continued down the hallway through the steel door that led to the cave. I could hear the commotion from the glass room in the distance.

"We only have a few minutes before they reach us."

"That'll be just enough time," said Mom as she unscrewed the vaulted door. We reached the precipice and peered over the ledge. Standing at the bottom were forty-seven villagers from Mori and Tavi's tribe. Dad, Sergio, Tavi, José, and Mom's pilot were off to the side. Tavi and Mori put their hands in the air with their fingers curled in, and silently the villagers did the same. Mom waved, and Dad and José waved back.

We began to climb down Mori's vine. I went first, then Mom, and then Mori who kept watch on the door for an attack. Mom had become much stronger now that she had a few sips of the formula and slid down the vine with ease. Dad reached out to her and held her tight.

"I'm so happy you're okay," Dad said.

"I'm fine, honey. Are you all alright?" she asked.

Dad nodded, and Mom hugged Sergio so tight that he couldn't breathe.

"Mom, I… need… air," he said, gasping.

When I reached the ground, we had a group hug, and the pilot and José shook Mom's hand. "Welcome back, Dione," said José. "We all missed you."

"Thanks for not giving up on me, José."

"You are most welcome," he said.

"Nice job, little man," I said, nudging Sergio.

He nudged me back and said, "Not too shabby. So, now that you can do some mindreading yourself, we probably can get into all sorts of trouble back home." He gave me an exaggerated wink.

We helped Dad up and he hobbled towards the water. Just then, the steel door swung open and the guards jumped onto the elevator. One pressed the keypad and it slowly lowered the men to the ground.

"Deep breaths now," Mom said.

They all took a deep breath dove into the ice-cold water. Sergio and I lingered for a moment to wrap the rest of the brown powder in the graviola leaf and tossed it onto the water's surface. We dove in quickly as the powder smoked. From a few feet under the water, I stopped swimming to gaze upward and saw large flames dancing on the water. Nothing, not even the bats, could get through that.

We swam through the dark waters and prayed that it was daytime. My heart sank as I feared that we would never find the opening if there was no light. But there was a dull light getting brighter and brighter as we swam towards it. I reached while every stroke had become harder and harder and my lungs ached. I saw my father swimming in front of me. His broken leg slowed him down. He had begun to panic. His arms and legs flailed, and I was terrified. We were so close, only twenty feet or so, and we'd be on the surface. Mom, Sergio, and I tried to pull Dad but we weren't strong enough. He was weakening and I could only see the white of his eyes. Tavi and Mori dove back in and scooped our father up quickly and pulled him to the surface. We came up and gasped for air. We all coughed and choked until we could breathe normally. Dad was unconscious and was lying by the water's edge.

Chapter 10
Coming Home

I closed my eyes tight and prayed. Dad was alright. I could hear him cough and wheeze but I kept my eyes closed. Mom pulled me close to her and hugged me for a long time while Dad caught his breath. "He's alright," she said.

I knew as soon as the fire was squelched, the bats would be after us again. We headed toward the village as quickly as we could. My father hobbled with his injured leg but Mori and Tavi were strong and Dad leaned on them for support. The villagers were very weak and moved as quickly as they could but were clearly exhausted.

We must have been only minutes from the village when the bats' shrieks could be heard. The adults scattered and hid under the lean-tos, pulling down the camouflage covering. My family hovered down in the brush. The children formed a circle in a clearing with their backs to one another. They joined hands and waited for their attackers. Sergio and I looked at each other, and in an instant, we broke free from our parents and headed for the circle.

"Wait. Stop!" Mom cried.

"Come back!" Dad said.

"It'll be okay!" Sergio yelled back.

They watched us in horror. Sergio and I joined the circle and clasped hands with Mori and Tavi. We waited silently. Mori leaned into me and whispered, "Sergio is your guide but you are the key, Larissa."

"What key? What do you mean?"

"We have been waiting for you too, Larissa," Mori said, handing me a soft piece of animal skin. I unfolded it quickly to find a drawing of my own face created with a single delicate line. The piece of leather looked very old. "My grandmother made it."

Tavi faced Sergio. "We cannot do this without either one of you. You complete this circle."

"You can talk to the bats. You can ask them to never return," Mori said.

"I can't do that. He can," I pointed toward the boy who had subdued the bat we trapped days before.

"You are stronger," said Mori. "You can control them. Send them back to their home permanently. They will listen to you."

"I… I can't."

"Yes, you can, Larissa. I will help you," Sergio said.

My brother pulled my hand gently into the center of the circle. I heard our mother gasp. I was shaking uncontrollably and tears streamed from my eyes. "I'm not strong enough."

"Yes, you are," he said. "You really are."

A bat swooped down and a second one followed. The children's hands were clenched tightly as they raised their arms high. Sergio grabbed my other hand and we too raised our hands high. We closed our eyes tight and for the first time, I believed that I could be strong. Though my eyes were closed, bright, colorful lights danced inside my eyelids. Bats shrieked while bursts of colorful lights exploded all around us. When I finally opened my eyes, a beautiful haze of purple and blue light had risen up over our heads and encircled the black beasts. They were caught up in the mist and flipped over gently. They no longer flapped their massive wings. They just floated.

I closed my eyes again all the while Sergio had been whispering, "Calm them. Tell them we will not hurt them."

"They're listening." Tavi whispered. "Ease their mind."

There was no sound, no chirping of crickets, no monkeys howling nor frogs croaking, nothing... but silence. My eyes opened and the bats were nestled on the ground, sleeping and silent. I walked through the circle of children, and without fear I unlocked the collars around their necks. I tossed the contraptions aside and quietly we collected our families and headed toward the village, leaving the bats to awaken on their own.

Our father always taught us never to be proud but it was alright to take pride in what you've accomplished; and that I did. I think we all felt deeply satisfied and happy. The villagers were free. Once the scientists learn that the bats had all been freed and cannot be controlled, they will know that the villagers had gained back their power. The families headed back to their dwellings and slept. Even Tavi slept. Our hunger would wait until morning. I slept without dreaming and it was a relief. I don't think I'll ever want to dream again. Of course, that would be impossible but I can do without premonitions for a while. Sergio, on the other hand, was raring to go. His *poderes* were new and exciting and he loved to talk to the villagers. The next morning, we

108

gathered for a celebration. It was amazing to see my parents together again. I've seen them hug a thousand times before but this one was the most meaningful to me.

We discussed our adventure all morning. Every moment was savored. Mom explained that she had learned many years ago, when Sergio and I were just babies, that there was a secret village deep in the Amazon. Most believed it was a folktale but the older Caboclos believed it to be true. They spoke of their ancestors who chased their families away because of their fear. They were very superstitious people. They believed that rain came when rain was needed and fish came when they were hungry, but to have powers like this could only be a curse for the village. It was believed to be unnatural. They felt that no human should ever wield such power. They saw it as humans taking advantage of nature.

"Why do we have this power, these *poderes*?"

Sergio and I turned from Mom's smiling face to Dad's.

"This is our family. My mother, your grandmother, was born and raised in this tribe," Mom said.

"Why did she leave?"

"She had been fishing outside the village and your grandfather's canoe had sailed up onto the rocks. He had been injured from a fall and he could not paddle back up the river. Your grandmother nursed him back to health and took him back to his own village, the Xingavi tribe, where they could continue treating him. She knew that she could never go back to her own village and risk the safety of her own tribe, so she remained with him and they fell in love," Mom explained.

Tavi and Mori joined us and offered us food. We realized how hungry we were and began to eat without taking our eyes off Mom or Dad. Music was heard as the villagers talked and ate but it was like a distant buzz. I could focus only on our conversation and tuned the world out.

"We're related to the villagers?"

"Yes, honey, they are your family," Mom said. "I never knew much about where my ancestors were from beyond my own parents. I just assumed your grandmother was a Caboclo like your grandfather. One day while I was working with the Xingavi tribe, a very old man had shown me the medicinal qualities of a rare and exotic plant. He poured a few drops into a woman's mouth who had been suffering from fatigue. Within minutes she was strong and healthy. I couldn't imagine something working that fast and asked to see how it was made. He took out the ingredients, nothing too exotic except for a white dried-up herb. I had never seen it before. He said he learned about the secrets of this white herb long ago from a beautiful girl who traveled down a river with an injured boy who had been his brother."

"So you've been getting the herbs from your own uncle?"

"You got it! He said that the beautiful woman taught him how the plant was grown and how to use it properly. He promised to keep the flower a secret and was only allowed to share the herb with a modern medicine woman who will arrive some day in the future," Mom said.

"They've been waiting for you too?" Sergio asked in disbelief. She smiled and nodded.

"He told me that he was my uncle, my father's brother. I didn't believe him until he explained who the mysterious woman was and the man she married. My parents left the Amazon together and lived in Rio de Janeiro where I was born. Both tribes knew about me. My own mother knew I'd return to help her people someday."

"Why didn't grandmother tell you about her village and your destiny to help the people?"

"They couldn't reveal anything about the village, just as I haven't revealed its secrets to you," Mom said. "My uncle explained to me that I must find my family. He had never seen the hidden village but knew that it existed. I started searching fourteen years ago but had very little luck. I searched for years, each time I came to Brazil.

"Finally," she said, "I found them. It wasn't easy through the dense foliage but in a small clearing I caught a glimpse of a girl. I copied the coordinates but the plane malfunctioned and we crashed. Tavi and Mori found me as if they had been waiting for me. They carried me to their hidden village. Mori's mother healed me before she was captured. I only spent a short time with them but it was a wonderful experience, one that I hoped to share with you all someday.

"The scientists robbed, spied on, and eventually kidnapped the people of this village. The villagers feared for their children, so they moved their village every few years to remote places but were eventually discovered. I had searched for so long but could not find them until Mori's mother sent me a map through my uncle. When I finally got close, my plane malfunctioned and crashed. My pilot was captured by a bat and I was hurt and too weak to travel, so I could not contact anyone. The villagers told me about the bats and the abductions. More and more adults disappeared each day. They lived in constant fear. When the last parent was kidnapped, I decided to allow myself the same fate so I could find them and somehow help them."

"So why was the flower so important? Does it really give power?"

"No." mom chuckled. "The flower is important to the villagers because they do not have the vitamins that we could get in our diet. But to us, it's nothing more than a protein shake. It gives you the proper supply of vitamins and minerals you need in a day, with a kick. That's why you and your brother are hardly ever ill."

I thought for a long time about that one. I realized that each night I was sick was the result of too much candy the day after Halloween and Christmas, and also from the time Sergio and I drank some concoction of mustard, ketchup, bananas, spaghetti, and lemonade.

"So why did we let them think the flower was so important?"

"I can answer that one," Sergio said. "If the scientists believed that the flower had properties that would give super-human abilities, even if it was untrue, it would keep them focused on the flower more than the villagers."

"That's right, honey," Mom said. "The truth is that your ancestors have these abilities that are embedded in their genes – *your* genes."

"Your mother has passed these genes onto you and your brother," Dad said. "The flower was just a decoy so they would not experiment on the villagers' anatomy."

"Mom, were you behind the curtain at the compound?" I asked.

"I was. You were reading my mind perfectly. It was exciting to see what you could do."

"Why couldn't the adults get away? Why couldn't they use their *poderes*?" I asked.

"The scientists didn't realize that the adult *poderes* weaken as the years progress. They thought the adults were careful about hiding their secrets better than the children, but they were wrong. That's why I can no longer hear the way you hear, Larissa. I used to be able to read minds too, but now I can only transfer thoughts occasionally." Mom turned to my father and said, "That's how I was able to transfer a message to you, Luca, so you could tell Larissa to find the flower. I wanted to exaggerate the flower's importance by keeping it hidden from them," she said.

"How did you even know I was in the compound?" Dad asked.

"Woman's intuition," she said playfully.

"How did you know *I* could read your mind? I never knew myself!" I asked.

"Because you are my daughter. If I was able to do this at one time, it is most likely you and Sergio could as well. The whole village could do it. That's how they communicate at nighttime. And... that's how I knew your father loved me. He constantly watched me and I always knew what he was thinking," she teased.

"Ugh," Sergio said, rolling his eyes.

"So Tavi and Mori are... my cousins?"

"Yes, they are," she said. She hugged Mori and Tavi who were smiling.

"But Mom, the scientists know where the village is and when they realize that the white flower is powerless, won't they come back?"

"No," she said, biting into a mango. "Their work is finished. The experiments went on for too long and they've run out of money. It was all run by a single man, a billionaire looking for more power. He was greedy and used all of his savings on the lab and the work. But it's over now. He will find out within a day or two that he is no more powerful than… your father."

"Thanks a lot," Dad said, laughing.

We all laughed. It was nice to see the people of the village truly happy and the children were playing again. The sun set but the music played on. No one feared the darkness anymore. The bats returned to the safety of their caves and will never be a threat again. The villagers knew that they would have to keep moving time and time again to secret, remote places to keep out of the public eye. Once the world learned about the compound, they would lose any sense of privacy.

We left the village a few days later and we promised to visit someday. Mom and Tavi's mother agreed to contact each other through the Xingavi tribe. They were an understanding and knowledgeable tribe who would help the villagers when in need.

We traveled back to the Zodiac. It took two and a half days to finally reach the channel where we left the fishing boat. But it could have taken forever for all I cared. My family was together and that's all I needed. José and Mom's pilot pushed off and we passed the time with stories of the Amazon tribes and their tales of an ancient village who disappeared from the world. Some of the stories were folk tales, of course, but it was fun to hear them anyway.

My parents took us back to visit Brazil two more times after that but we never visited the village again. It was too difficult and risky to travel that deep into the Amazon. The villagers moved their location and we felt it best to give them their anonymity. I often think about Mori and Tavi. I think about their haunting eyes and their painted bodies. I missed our family and I felt a bit of emptiness in my heart since the day we had left the village.

It's been five years since our mother's plane had gone down in the jungle. We hadn't talked about our adventure past the first year and I wonder how much my family truly remembers. My mother has blocked out some of it but I recall every moment. We decided to spend the last summer together before I started college. I was going to study anthropology, hoping to discover more about the villages in the Amazon. It was all so fascinating to learn about different cultures that are so unlike the life I live in the United States. Who would have guessed that I'd be related to a village that had been hidden for a century? Those days in the Amazon will never be forgotten.

As for Sergio, he will graduate high school next year, two years earlier than his peers. He doesn't mind leaving his friends behind and is thrilled to be entering the world of academia where he has been offered a scholarship in biology, of course.

We don't use our *poderes* anymore; they have gotten weaker and are somewhat unreliable. Mom and Dad always said that our adventure had matured us, maybe too much, and we found it difficult settling into our old lives again. We managed and found comfort in one another's company.

If you're wondering what happened to the compound, a billionaire, Dr. Gabriel Reinhardt, went belly-up when his thirty-two-year research project fell apart. The compound was investigated and the police released the animals back into the wild. All of the journals written about the village and the white flower were burned by Dr. Reinhardt himself before the government could confiscate it. I suppose he didn't want anyone to learn that he was responsible for kidnapping and illegal experimentation. Dr. Reinhardt is living the rest of his life behind bars along with his accomplices. I took solace in knowing there was one less criminal in the world to worry about.

One particular evening, on my mother's birthday, the doorbell rang at half past nine. I answered the door while my family played a game of speed scrabble. A small package was left on the doorstep as a truck sped off. I took a deep breath and tried to hold on to the refreshing, warm summer breeze. The package was written with a neat hand but had no return address. I ripped it open and inside was a small leather pouch. I opened it slowly and saw something inside that took my breath away. It was a flattened, perfectly preserved white flower. The sweet aroma of cotton candy filled the air and dissipated. Beneath the flower was a small piece of animal skin. On one side, a tiny detailed map drawn with a single line was delicately designed. On the other side was a beautifully written note written in English. It simply read, *"When will you be coming home?"*

Tears streamed from my eyes. I never realized how much my heart ached for my new family. I knew that the village must now be in contact with Mom's Caboclo friends in order to get this package to us.

Sergio, Mom, Dad, and I boarded a plane two days later and headed back to our family in the Amazon. We followed the map and found our village hidden even deeper and in an even more remote location in the depths of the rainforest. We reached the village to find Tavi and Mori, who were adults now with children of their own. We greeted one another in their traditional way and they greeted us in ours. We spent the evenings around the fire, talking, dancing, and playing charades, a game they continued to play even after we were gone. That was when I realized that my happiest moments were times spent with family.